"You want a simple divorce. Which you can have—at a price."

"That's blackmail." Kate's voice shook.

"Is it?" he said. "But perhaps I do not agree that our marriage has 'irretrievably broken down,' as you allege."

Kate drew a deep breath. "You're bluffing. You don't wish to stay married any more than I do."

His mouth twisted. "You're mistaken, *agapi mou*. I am in no particular hurry to be free."

SARA CRAVEN was born in South Devon, England, and grew up surrounded by books, in a house by the sea. After leaving grammar school she worked as a local journalist, covering everything from flower shows to murders. She started writing for Harlequin Mills & Boon® in 1975. Apart from writing, her passions include films, music, cooking and eating in good restaurants. She now lives in Somerset.

Sara Craven has recently become the latest (and last ever) winner of the British quiz show *Mastermind*.

Books by Sara Craven

HARLEQUIN PRESENTS®

2119—BARTALDI'S BRIDE
2155—MARRIAGE BY DECEPTION
2192—THE TYCOON'S MISTRESS
2240—ROME'S REVENGE

Don't miss any of our special offers. Write to us at the following address for information on our newest releases.

Harlequin Reader Service
U.S.: 3010 Walden Ave., P.O. Box 1325, Buffalo, NY 14269
Canadian: P.O. Box 609, Fort Erie, Ont. L2A 5X3

Sara Craven

SMOKESCREEN MARRIAGE

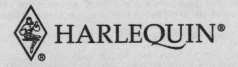

HARLEQUIN®

TORONTO • NEW YORK • LONDON
AMSTERDAM • PARIS • SYDNEY • HAMBURG
STOCKHOLM • ATHENS • TOKYO • MILAN • MADRID
PRAGUE • WARSAW • BUDAPEST • AUCKLAND

ISBN 0-373-12287-X

SMOKESCREEN MARRIAGE

First North American Publication 2002.

CHAPTER ONE

THE room was in deep shadow. Moonlight pouring through the slats of the tall shuttered windows lay in thin bands across the tiled floor.

The whirr of the ceiling fan gently moving the warm air above the wide bed was barely audible against the ceaseless rasp of the cicadas in the garden below the room.

Once, she'd found these sounds alien. Now, they were the natural accompaniment to her nights in this house.

As was the firm masculine tread approaching the bed. The warm, husky voice, touched with laughter, whispering 'Katharina *mou*.'

And she, turning slowly, languidly, under the linen sheet that was her only covering, smiling her welcome, as she reached up to him with outstretched arms, her body alive with need—with longing...

With a gasp, Kate sat up in the darkness, throat tight, heart pounding violently.

She made herself draw deep calming breaths as she glanced round the room, seeking reassurance. Her bedroom, in her flat. Curtains masking the windows, not shutters. And, outside, the uneasy rumble of London traffic.

A dream, she thought. Only a bad dream. Just another nightmare.

At the beginning, they'd been almost nightly occurrences, as her stunned mind and bruised senses tried to rationalise what had happened to her.

She had never really succeeded, of course. The hurt, the betrayal had cut too deep. The events of the past year were always there, in the corner of her mind, eating corrosively into her consciousness.

5

But the bad dreams had been kept at bay for a while. It was now almost two weeks since the last one.

She had, she thought, begun to heal.

And now this…

Was it an omen? she wondered. Tomorrow—the next day—would there be some news at last? The letter—the phone call—that would bring her the promise of freedom.

God knows, she'd made it as easy as she could, going right against the advice of her lawyer.

'But, Mrs Theodakis, you're entitled…'

She'd stopped him there. 'I want nothing,' she said. 'Nothing at all. Kindly make sure the other side is—aware of that. And please don't use that name either,' she added constrainedly. 'I prefer Miss Dennison.'

He had assented politely, but his raised brows told her more loudly than words that no amount of preference could change a thing.

She had taken off her wedding ring, but she couldn't as easily erase the events of the past year from her tired memory.

She was still legally the wife of Michael Theodakis, and would remain so until she received his consent to the swift, clean-break divorce she had requested.

Once she was free of him, then the nightmares would stop, she told herself. And she could begin to put her life back together again.

That was the inner promise that had kept her going through these dark days and endless nights since she'd fled from Mick, and their charade of a marriage. From the images that still haunted her, waking and sleeping.

She drew her knees up to her chin, shivering a little. Her cotton nightgown was damp, and clinging to her body. She was tired—her job as a tour guide escorting parties of foreign tourists round the British Isles was a demanding one—but her body was wide awake, restless with the needs and desires she'd struggled so hard to suppress.

How could the memory of him still be so potent? she wondered despairingly. Why couldn't she forget him as easily as he seemed to have forgotten her? Why didn't he answer her solicitor's letters—or instruct one of the team of lawyers who served the mighty Theodakis clan to deal with them for him?

With all his money and power, it was the simplest thing in the world to rid himself of an unwanted wife. He was signing papers all day long. What would one more signature matter?

She lay down again, pulling the covers round her, in spite of the warmth of the August night. Cocooning herself so that the expanse of the bed beside her would not seem quite so empty—so desolate.

And knowing that nothing would ever make any difference to the loneliness and the hurt.

It was nearly eight when she reached home the following evening, and Kate felt bone-weary as she let herself into the narrow hall. She had spent the day showing a party of thirty Japanese tourists round Stratford-on-Avon. They had been unfailingly polite, and interested, absorbing information like sponges, but Kate was aware that she had not been on top form. She'd been restless, edgy all day, blaming her disturbed night for her difficulties in concentration.

Tonight, she thought grimly, she would take one of the pills the doctor had prescribed when she first returned from Greece.

She needed this job, and couldn't afford to lose it, even if it was only temporary, filling in for someone on maternity leave.

All the winter jobs for reps with tour companies had already gone when she came back to Britain, although her old company Halcyon Club Travel were keen to hire her again next summer.

And that's what she planned to do, although she'd stipulated that she would not return to any of the Greek islands.

On her way to the stairs, she paused to collect her mail from the row of rickety pigeon-holes on the wall.

Mostly circulars, she judged, and the gas bill—and then stopped, her attention totally arrested as she saw the Greek stamp.

She stared down at the large square envelope with its neatly typed direction, her eyes dilating, a small choked sound rising in her throat.

She thought, 'He's found me. He knows where I am. But how?'

And why was he making contact with her directly, when she'd made it clear that all correspondence was to be conducted through their lawyers?

But then, when had Mick Theodakis ever played by any rules except his own?

She went up the stairs slowly, aware that her legs were shaking. When she reached her door, she had to struggle to fit her key into the lock, but at last she managed it.

In her small living room, she dropped the letter on to the dining table as if it was red-hot, then walked across to her answerphone which was blinking at her, and pressed the 'play' button. Perhaps, if Mick had written to her, he'd also contacted her lawyer, and the message she was hoping for might be waiting at last.

Instead Grant's concerned voice said, 'Kate—are you all right? You haven't called me this week. Touch base, darling—please.'

Kate sighed inwardly, and went across to the bedroom to take off the navy shift dress, and navy and emerald striped blazer that constituted her uniform.

It was kind of Grant to be anxious, but she knew in her heart that it was more than kindness that prompted his frequent calls. It was pressure. He wanted her back, their former relationship re-established, and moved on to the next stage. He took it for granted that she wanted this too. That, like him, she regarded the past year as an aberration—a period of temporary insanity, now happily concluded. And that when she had gained her divorce, she would marry him.

But Kate knew it would never happen. She and Grant had not been officially engaged, when she'd gone off to work as a travel company rep on Zycos in the Ionian Sea, but she knew, when the season was over, he would ask her to marry him, and that she would probably agree.

She hadn't even been sure why she was hesitating. He was good-looking, they shared a number of interests, and, if his kisses did not set her on fire, Kate enjoyed them enough to look forward to the full consummation of their relationship. And during her weeks on Zycos she had missed him, written to him every week, and happily anticipated his phone calls planning their future.

Surely that was a good enough basis for marriage—wasn't it?

Probably Grant thought it still was. Only she knew better. Knew she was no longer the same person. And soon she would have to tell him so, she thought with genuine regret.

She unzipped her dress, and put it on a hanger. Underneath she was wearing bra and briefs in white broderie anglaise, pretty and practical, but not glamorous or sexy, she thought, studying herself dispassionately.

And totally different from the exquisite lingerie that Mick had brought her from Paris and Rome—lacy cobwebby things that whispered against her skin. Filmy enticing scraps to please the eyes of a lover.

Only, there was no lover—and never had been.

She slipped on her pale-green gingham housecoat and tied its sash, then put up a hand and removed the barrette that confined her red-gold hair at the nape of her neck during the working day, letting it cascade down to her shoulders.

'Like a scented flame,' Mick would tell her huskily, his hands tangling in the silky strands—lifting them to his lips.

She stiffened, recognising that was a no-go area. She could not afford such memories.

She wanted to move away from the mirror but something kept her there, examining herself with cold critical attention.

How could she ever have imagined in her wildest dreams that she was the kind of woman to attract and hold a man like Mick Theodakis? she asked herself bleakly.

Because she had never been a classic beauty. Her nose was too long and her jaw too square for that. But she had good cheekbones, and long lashes, although the eyes they fringed were an odd shade between green and grey.

'Jade smoke,' Mick had called them...

And she was luckier than most redheads, she thought, swiftly refocusing her attention. Her creamy skin didn't burn or freckle, but turned a light, even gold. The tan she'd acquired in Greece still lingered. She could see quite plainly the white band of her finger where her wedding ring had been. But that was the only mark, because Mick had always encouraged her to join him in sunbathing nude beside their private pool.

She froze, cursing inwardly. Oh, God, why was she doing this to herself—allowing herself to remember these things?

Well, she knew why, of course. It was because of that envelope ticking away like a time bomb in the other room.

Her throat tightened uncontrollably. She turned away from the mirror and went into the kitchen and made herself a mug of coffee, hot, black and very strong. If she'd had any brandy, she'd have added a dollop of that too.

Then, she sat down at the table, and steeled herself to open the envelope.

It was disturbing to realise how easily he'd been able to pinpoint her whereabouts—as if he was demonstrating his power over her from across the world. Showing her that there was nowhere she could run and hide. No refuge that he could not find.

Only he had no power, she told herself fiercely. Not any more. Not ever again. And she tore open the envelope.

She found herself staring down at an elegantly engraved

white card. A wedding invitation, she thought in total bewilderment, as she scanned it. And the last thing she'd expected to find. She felt oddly deflated as she read the beau-
tifully printed words.

So—Ismene, Mick's younger sister was marrying her
Petros at last. But why on earth was she being sent an invitation?

Frowningly, she unfolded the accompanying note.

'Dearest Katharina,' it read. 'Papa finally gave his permission and I am so happy. We are to be married in the village
in October, and you promised you would be there for me on
my wedding day. I depend on you, sister. Your loving
Ismene.'

Kate crumpled the note in her hand. Was Ismene crazy, or
just naïve? she wondered. She couldn't really expect her
brother's estranged wife to be part of a family occasion,
whatever rash commitment Kate might have made in those
early days when she was still living in her fool's paradise.

But I'm not that person any more, Kate thought, her face
set, her body rigid. I'll have to write to her—explain somehow.

But why had Mick ever allowed the invitation to be sent?
It made no sense. Although the wilful Ismene probably
hadn't bothered to seek his permission, she acknowledged
with a faint sigh.

And she was astonished that Aristotle Theodakis, the all-
powerful patriarch of the family, had agreed to the marriage.
While she'd been living under his roof at the Villa Dionysius,
he'd been adamantly opposed to it. No mere doctor was good
enough for his daughter, he'd roared, even if it was the son
of his old friend and *tavli* opponent. And slammed doors,
furious scenes, and the sound of Ismene's hysterical weeping
had been almost daily occurrences.

Until Mick had flatly announced he could stand no more,
and had insisted that he and Kate move out of their wing of

the main building, and out of earshot, down to the comparative seclusion of the beach house. Where they'd remained...

She drank some of the scalding coffee, but it did nothing to melt the ice in the pit of her stomach.

Those weeks, she thought, had been the happiest of her life. Day had succeeded sunlit day. Night followed moonlit night. Raised voices were replaced by birdsong, the whisper of the breeze in the pine trees, and the murmur of the sea.

And, above all, Michael touching her—whispering to her, coaxing her out of the last of her natural shyness, teaching her to take as well as give in their lovemaking. And to be proud of her slim, long-legged body with its narrow waist and small high breasts.

And she'd been an eager pupil, she thought bitterly. How readily she'd surrendered to the caress of his cool, experienced hands and mouth, sobbing out her breathless, mindless rapture as their naked bodies joined in passion.

So beguiled, so entranced by the new sensual vistas that Mick had revealed to her, that she'd mistaken them for love.

Whereas all she'd really been to him was a novelty—a temporary amusement.

The smokescreen he'd cynically needed to divert attention from his real passion.

The coffee tasted bitter, and she pushed it away from her, feeling faintly nauseous.

She couldn't afford to tear her heart out over Ismene, she told herself curtly. They'd become close over the months, and she knew that the younger girl would be missing her company with only Victorine to turn to. In fact, the note had almost sounded like a cry for help.

But she couldn't allow herself to think like that. And in particular she couldn't permit her mind to dwell on Victorine, the Creole beauty who now ruled Aristotle Theodakis, without releasing any of her hold over his son.

She would write a brief and formal expression of regret,

and leave it there. Keep it strictly impersonal, although Ismene might be hurt to have no response to her note.

But then, Kate thought, I also have the right to some reaction to my request for a divorce. After all, it's been a month since my lawyer sent off the papers.

Impatiently, she pushed the invitation away and rose. It was no wonder she was feeling flaky. She ought to have something to eat. She'd only had time to grab a sandwich at lunch time, and there was cold chicken and salad in the fridge, only her appetite seemed to have deserted her.

And she had a hectic day tomorrow—a group of reluctant French schoolchildren to chivvy around the Tower of London.

Perhaps she would just have a warm shower, wash her hair, and go to bed early. Catch up on some of that lost sleep.

Her bathroom was small, and the shower cubicle rather cramped, not tempting her to linger. She towelled down quickly, and resumed her housecoat before returning to the living room with her hair-drier.

She was just plugging it in when, to her surprise and irritation, someone knocked at the door.

Kate sighed, winding a towel round her wet hair. It was bound to be Mrs Thursgood, the elderly widow who lived on the ground floor, and accepted parcels and packets intended for other tenants who'd left for work before the mail arrived.

She was a kindly soul but gossipy, and she would expect a cup of tea and a cosy chat in return for her trouble of trailing up to the top floor with Kate's book club selection, or whatever.

I really, truly, don't want to talk, Kate thought grimly, as she pinned on a smile and flung open the door.

And stood, lips parting in a soundless gasp, eyes widening in shock, feeling the blood drain from her face.

'My beloved wife,' Michael Theodakis said softly. '*Kalispera*. May I come in?'

'No,' she said. Her voice sounded hoarse—distorted above the sudden roaring in her ears. She was afraid she was going to faint, and knew she couldn't afford any such weakness. She took a step backwards.

'No,' she repeated more vehemently.

He was smiling, totally at ease, propping a dark-clad shoulder against the doorframe.

'But we cannot conduct a civilised conversation on the *door*step, *agapi mou*.'

She said thickly, 'I've got nothing to say to you—on the doorstep or anywhere else. If you want to talk, speak to my solicitor. And don't call me your darling.'

'How unkind,' he said. 'When I have travelled such a long way at such inconvenience to see you again. I'd hoped some of our Greek hospitality might have rubbed off on you.'

'That isn't the aspect of my life with you that I remember most clearly,' Kate said, her breathing beginning to steady. 'And I didn't invite you here, so please go.'

Mick Theodakis raised both hands in mock surrender. 'Easy, Katharina *mou*. I did not come here to fight a war, but negotiate a peaceful settlement. Isn't that what you want too?'

'I want a quick divorce,' she said. 'And never to see you again.'

'Go on.' The dark eyes glinted down at her from beneath hooded lids. 'Surely you have a third wish. All the best stories do, I believe.'

Kate drew a quick, sharp breath. 'This,' she said gratingly, 'is not a fairy story.'

'No,' he said. 'To be honest, I am not sure whether it is a comedy or a tragedy.'

'Honest?' Kate echoed scornfully. 'You don't know the meaning of the word.'

'However,' he went on as if she hadn't spoken. 'I am quite certain I am not leaving until you have heard what I have to say, *yineka mou*.'

'I am not your wife,' she said. 'I resigned that dubious honour when I left Kefalonia. And I thought I'd made it clear in my note that our so-called marriage was over.'

'It was a model of clarity,' he said courteously. 'I have learned every word of it by heart. And the fact that you left your wedding ring beside it added extra emphasis.'

'Then you'll understand there is nothing to discuss.' She lifted her chin. 'Now, go please. I have a heavy duty tomorrow, and I'd like to go to bed.'

'Not,' he said softly. 'With wet hair. That is something that *I* remember from our brief marriage, Katharina.' He stepped into the room, kicking the door shut behind him.

There was no lock on her bedroom door, and one dodgy bolt on the bathroom. With nowhere to run, Kate decided to stand her ground.

'How dare you.' Her face was burning as she glared at him. 'Get out of here, before I call the police.'

'To do what?' Mick asked coolly. 'Have I ever struck you—or molested you in any way, *agapi mou*, that you did not welcome?' He watched the colour suddenly deepen in her shocked face, and nodded sardonically. 'Besides, all police are reluctant to intervene in domestic disputes. So, why don't you sit down and dry your hair while you listen to what I have to say?'

He paused, then held out his hand. 'Unless you would like me to dry it for you,' he added softly. 'As I used to.'

Kate swallowed convulsively, and shook her head, not trusting her voice.

It wasn't fair, she raged inwardly. It wasn't right for him to remind her of all the small, tender intimacies they'd once shared.

The way she'd sat between his knees as he blow-dried her hair, combing it gently with his fingers, letting the soft strands drift in the current of warm air.

And how her efforts to perform the same service for him had always been thwarted, as he loosened the sash on her robe, and drew the folds slowly apart, pressing tiny sensuous kisses on her naked body as she stood, flushed and breathless, in front of him. Until her attempt at hairdressing was forgotten in the sweet urgency of the moment.

Oh, she did not need to remember that.

Her cotton housecoat was long-sleeved and full-skirted, buttoned chastely to the throat, but she was still blazingly aware that she was naked under it—and that he knew it too, and was enjoying her discomfort.

The room seemed suddenly to have shrunk. His presence dominated it, physically and emotionally. Invaded her space in the worst way. Dried her throat and made her legs shake under her.

Even as she turned away and walked across to the dining table, every detail of him was etched on her mind, as if she'd touched him with her fingers.

Yet she did not have to do that—to remember.

She knew that the black curling hair was brushed back from his face with careless elegance. That his dark eyes were brilliant, but watchful beneath their heavy lids, or that the cool, firm mouth held a hint of sensuality in the slight fullness of the lower lip.

It was a proud face, strong and uncompromising, but when he smiled, its charm had twisted the heart in her body.

He was formally dressed, the charcoal business suit accentuating the tall, lean body which moved with such arrogant grace. His olive skin looked very dark against the immaculate white shirt. His tie was silk, and there were discreet gold links in his cuffs matching the narrow bracelet on his watch and, she noticed with a sudden painful thud of her heart, the plain band on the third finger of his right hand.

The ring which matched hers, inscribed inside with their names and the date, which she had slipped on to his finger on their wedding day...

How could he still be wearing it? How could he be such a hypocrite? she asked herself numbly.

He said, 'Aren't you going to ask me to sit down—offer me some coffee?'

'You're not a guest,' Kate said, keeping her voice level with an effort. 'And this is not a social call.' She frowned. 'How did you get in, anyway?'

'A charming lady on the ground floor.' He paused. 'She seemed pleased you were having a visitor.'

Mrs Thursgood, Kate thought, grinding her teeth. Who normally guarded the front door like Cerberus at the gates of Hell.

She said, 'She allows her imagination to run away with her sometimes.'

She loosened the towel that was swathed round her head, and her damp hair tumbled on to her shoulders. Then she switched on the drier, and picked up the brush.

Mick stood by the old-fashioned fireplace watching every movement, his whole body very still, except for a muscle flickering at the side of his mouth.

He said at last, 'You've received Ismene's invitation.' His tone was abrupt, and it was a statement rather than a question.

'It came today.'

'So you haven't had time to reply.'

'It won't take much time,' Kate said shortly. 'Naturally, I shan't be going.'

'Ah,' Mick said gently. 'But that is what I came to discuss with you. It would mean a great deal to my sister to have you present, so I hope you will reconsider.'

Kate switched off the drier and stared at him, pushing her hair back from her face. 'That's impossible.'

'I hope not. Ismene has missed you very badly, and this is a special time for her.' He paused. 'I would regard your attendance as a favour.'

Kate gasped. 'And that's supposed to make all the difference?' she demanded furiously.

'I thought it might.' He leaned an arm on the mantelshelf,

looking hatefully assured and relaxed. 'In fact, I believed we might exchange favours.'

There was an uncertain silence, then Kate said, 'What do you mean?'

'You want a simple, consensual divorce.' He smiled at her. 'Which you can have—at a price.'

There was another tingling silence.

She said, 'And if the price is too high?'

He shrugged. 'Then I refuse to consent, and we let the legal process run its course.' He added casually, 'I understand it can take several years.'

'That's—blackmail.' Her voice shook.

'Is it?' he said. 'But perhaps I do not agree that our marriage has "irretrievably broken down" as you allege in that document.'

'But you must. It has.' Kate drew a deep breath. 'And you're bluffing. I know you are. You don't wish to stay married any more than I do.'

His mouth twisted. 'You're mistaken, *agapi mou*. I am in no particular hurry to be free.'

No, she thought, with a stab of anguish. Not while your father is still alive, and Victorine is nominally his...

She said slowly, 'So I have to attend Ismene's wedding if I want a quick divorce.'

'Is it really such a hardship? Kefalonia is very beautiful in September.'

'Kefalonia is beautiful all the year round.' Her tone was curt. 'It's only some of the people there who make it ugly.'

'A word of advice, *pedhi mou*.' His smile was mirthless. 'It is better to win an opponent over than to antagonise him.'

Kate lifted her chin. 'I think it's a little late to worry about that.' She hesitated. 'But everyone must know by now that our marriage is over. Won't they find it strange if I'm at the wedding?'

'I am not interested in what people think.' His voice was suddenly harsh. 'Besides, they only know that we have been separated for a short time. You might simply have come back to this country to attend to some family business.'

'Is that what you've been telling people?' She shook her head. 'My God, you can't even be honest about our marriage breaking down.'

'They will know soon enough, when the wedding is over.'

'Well, I hope you don't expect me to take part in some spurious reunion,' Kate said acidly. 'I'm not that good an actress.' She paused. 'Why do you want me there?'

'Did I say wanted?' Mick drawled. 'Don't flatter yourself, my sweet one. I am here on Ismene's behalf, not my own.'

She did not look at him, staring instead at her gingham-covered knee. 'Then I'd be there—just as an ordinary guest? Nothing more?'

He said mockingly, 'Why, Katharina, did you think you had left me all these weeks to sleep alone? That I've been burning for your return. What an innocent you are.'

'Not,' she said, 'any more.' She was silent for a moment. 'I need time to think about this.'

'You have twenty-four hours. I am staying at the Royal Empress Hotel. You remember it?'

'Yes.' It was a painful whisper.

He nodded. 'You can contact me there with your answer.'

He walked to the door, and paused for a final swift look round the room.

He said, 'So this is what you left me for. I hope it is worth it.'

'I don't have to live in the lap of luxury to be happy,' Kate said defiantly.

'Evidently,' he said. 'If happy is what you are.' He looked her over, slowly and thoroughly, a smile curling his mouth.

He said softly, 'Eyes like smoke and hair like flame. What a waste *agapi mou*. What a tragic waste.'

And was gone.

CHAPTER TWO

FOR several long moments Kate stood like a statue, staring at the closed door, pain and disbelief warring within her for supremacy.

Then she gave a little choked cry and ran to her bedroom, flinging herself face down across the bed, her hands gripping the covers as if they were her last hold on sanity.

She said aloud, 'Fool.' And again, more savagely, her voice breaking, '*Fool.*'

Had she really thought she could escape so easily? That Michael Theodakis would simply allow her—the girl he'd taken from nowhere—to walk away from him?

Not that he cared about her, or their marriage, as she had bitter cause to know, but the fact that she'd chosen to expose the hypocrisy of their relationship by leaving, had clearly damaged his pride. And that, of course, was an unforgivable sin.

Her own pride, naturally, didn't count.

He hadn't even asked her why she had left, but then he didn't have to. He already knew. He would have been told…

Nor had he offered one word of apology or explanation for the actions which had driven her away.

No, she was clearly the one who was at fault because she'd failed to turn a blind eye to his cynical infidelity.

After all, she'd had the Theodakis millions to enjoy, and she could not deny Mick had been generous. There'd been the house outside Athens, and the sumptuous apartments in Paris and New York as well as the clothes and jewellery he'd given her, all of which she'd left behind when she fled.

But that had been her choice, and Mick, no doubt, felt he

20

had bought her silence—her discretion, and, in his eyes, she had reneged on their unwritten bargain.

A bargain she had not realised existed until that terrible afternoon...

She shuddered, pressing her face deep into the bed until coloured sparks danced behind her closed eyelids.

But nothing could drive the image from her brain. Mick sprawled naked and asleep across the bed—their bed. And Victorine sitting at the dressing table combing her hair, clad in nothing but a towel.

And now, in spite of that, he required her to stand meekly at his side during Ismene's wedding celebrations, playing the dutiful wife. As if she owed him something.

But she'd only have to role-play by day, she reminded herself. At least she would not be asked to pretend at night.

And neither would he. Not any longer.

How could a man do that? she wondered wildly. How could he make love to one woman, with his heart and mind committed to another?

And all those precious passionate moments when the dark strength of his body had lifted her to the edge of paradise and beyond—how could they have meant so little to him?

But perhaps sexual fulfilment had also been part of his side of the bargain along with the designer wardrobe and the money he'd provided. One of the assets of being Mrs Michael Theodakis.

But it wasn't enough. Because she'd wanted love. And that was something he'd never offered. At least he'd been honest about that.

Probably, he'd found her inexperience—her naïvete amusing, she thought, lashing herself into fresh anger against him.

Because anger was good. Safe. It kept the frantic tears of loneliness and betrayal at bay. And she couldn't afford any more tears. Any more heartbreak.

She'd wept enough. Now, somehow, she had to move on. But she couldn't begin to build a new life while her brief marriage still existed, trapping her in the old one. She needed it to be over, and left far behind her. But for that, of course, she had to have Mick's co-operation. Oh, it would be so good to tell him to go to hell. That she would die sooner than return to Kefalonia and play at being his wife again for however short a time.

Because that meant she would become once more the smokescreen against his father's jealous and totally justified suspicions. And how could she bear it?

Or stand seeing, yet again, the triumph and contempt in Victorine's beautiful face? The look she'd turned on Kate, standing ashen-faced in the doorway that afternoon only a few agonised weeks ago.

'How tactless of you, *chère*.' Her honeyed drawl was barbed. 'Perhaps in future you should knock before entering your husband's bedroom.'

Kate had taken two shaky steps backwards, then run for the bathroom down the passage, her hand over her mouth as nausea churned inside her.

She was violently, cripplingly sick, kneeling on the tiled floor while walls and ceiling revolved unsteadily around her. She had no idea how long she'd stayed there. But eventually some firm purpose was born out of the sickness and misery, making her realise that she had to get out. That her brief marriage was over, and that she could not bear to spend even another hour under any roof that belonged to the Theodakis family.

She had to force herself to go back into that bedroom, bracing herself for another humiliating confrontation, but Victorine had gone.

Mick was still fast asleep. Exhausted by his labours, no doubt, she thought, rubbing salt into her own bitter wounds. And how dared he sleep while her heart was breaking?

She needed to confront him, she realised. To accuse him and see the guilt in his face.

She put her hand on his shoulder, and shook him.

'Mick.' Her voice cracked on his name. 'Wake up.'

He stirred drowsily, without opening his eyes. '*S'agapo*,' he muttered, his voice slurred. 'I love you.'

Kate gasped, and took a step backwards, a stricken hand flying to her mouth. At last he'd said them—the words she'd yearned to hear ever since they'd been together.

Only they were not meant for her, but his secret lover— the woman he'd been enjoying so passionately in her absence. The mistress he'd never actually discarded. It was the final—the unforgivable hurt, she thought as she turned painfully and walked away.

She packed the minimum in a small weekend case, then scribbled him a note which she left on the night table with her wedding ring.

'I should never have married you,' she wrote. 'It was a terrible mistake, and I cannot bear to go on living with you for another moment. Don't try to find me.'

No one saw her go. She drove to the airport, and managed to get a seat on a plane to Athens, and from there to London. She had sworn that she would never go back.

And I can't, Kate thought, a shudder crawling the length of her body. I can't do it. It's too degrading to have to face her. To see them together, knowing what I know.

But what real alternative did she have?

She couldn't wait for years in limbo until Mick finally decided to let her go.

And, while his father lived, he had no real reason to end the marriage.

She had humiliated him by her precipitate departure, and she was being punished as a consequence. That was what it was all about. She had to be returned to the scene of her anguish—her betrayal—and made to endure all the memories and misery that it would evoke.

She burrowed into the quilt like a small wounded animal seeking sanctuary, her mind rejecting the images forcing themselves relentlessly on her inner vision.

Oh, how could he do this? How dared he simply—appear in her life again and start making demands?

Because he's without shame, she told herself, bitterly. And without decency. He's rich enough to do without them.

But I'm not. And somehow I have to find my way through this, and keep my own integrity in the process. And lying here with my eyes shut isn't going to change a thing.

She sat up slowly, pushing her still-damp hair back from her face with a slight shiver.

Meanwhile she had a job to do tomorrow, and preparations to make for that. Normal life was there to be got on with, even if the safe wall she'd thought she'd built around herself had suddenly come crashing down.

She trailed back into the living room, and switched on her hair-drier, staring unseeingly into space as she dealt with the tangled red waves, restoring them to some kind of order.

As, in the fullness of time, she would restore her life. Find a new calm—a new security.

There had never been any safety with Mick, of course. He'd appeared on her horizon like some great dark planet, and she'd been the moon drawn helplessly into his orbit. And by the time she'd realised the danger she was in, it was already too late.

But from the first time she'd seen him, she'd been in too deep, out of her depth and sinking.

As the drier hummed, Kate let her tired mind drift back over the months to where it had all begun...

'Oh, come on, Katie, don't let me down. It'll be a laugh.' Lisa's tone was cajoling. 'After all, when do we get a chance to get inside a hotel like the Zycos Regina? Don't you want to see how the other half live? Besides, I really need you to make up the foursome.'

Kate bit her lip. It had been a long season on the Greek island of Zycos, and, although on the whole she'd enjoyed being a tour rep for Halcyon Club Travel, she felt bone-weary now that it was over.

All she wanted to do that evening was complete her packing for the following day's flight, have a hot shower, and an early night. But Lisa, the fellow rep with whom she'd shared a small apartment all summer, wanted a night on the town.

She said cautiously, 'Who did you say was going?'

'His name's Stavros,' Lisa said. 'And he's the disc jockey at the Nite Spot down on the waterfront.'

'Oh,' Kate said. 'That place.'

Lisa tossed her head. 'You're such a snob,' she accused.

Kate sighed. 'Not at all. It just hasn't got a very good reputation, and you know it. It's always being raided.'

'Well, we're not taking clients there,' Lisa said. 'And Stavros just plays the music. He's gorgeous.' She rolled her eyes lasciviously. 'The other guy's his cousin Dimitris from Athens.'

Kate began, 'I don't think...' but Lisa cut across her.

'Oh, come on, Katie. Let your hair down for once. It's an evening out, not a lifetime commitment, for God's sake. And we'll be out of here tomorrow.'

Well that was true, Kate acknowledged. It was just one evening, and she could always invent a diplomatic headache if things got heavy.

Besides, if she was honest, she'd always had a sneaking curiosity about the Zycos Regina, the largest but also most exclusive hotel on the island, and set in its own private grounds well away from the lively coastal resorts favoured by the majority of tourists.

She knew that it was part of a chain of equally prestigious hotels dotted round the Mediterranean, their standards of luxury and service putting them out of the reach of the package tour market.

It might be fun, she thought, not just to see how the other half lived, but join them too for a brief while.

She smiled at Lisa. 'All right,' she said. 'You talked me into it.'

She chose carefully from her limited wardrobe that evening, opting for a black linen shift, knee-length, sleeveless and discreetly square necked. Lisa, blonde and bubbly, favoured the outrageous look out of uniform, and would be wearing something skimpy and cut-off, but Kate felt that restraint was her best bet.

For that reason, she twisted her hair into its usual tidy pleat instead of leaving it loose on her shoulders, as she'd originally intended. And she applied just a modicum of makeup, darkening her long lashes, and applying a light coral glow to her mouth.

She slipped on a pair of strappy sandals, then stood back to view herself in the mirror.

The evening was warm and still, but she suddenly found herself shivering as if a small chill wind had penetrated the shutters of her room.

And heard a warning voice in her head say quietly, 'Be careful.'

Oh, for God's sake, she thought impatiently as she turned towards the door. What can possibly happen in such a public—and eminently high-class—place?

Stavros, she disliked on sight. His coarse good looks might attract Lisa, but held no appeal for her. He looked her up and down smilingly, and she felt as if she'd been touched by a finger dipped in slime.

And Dimitris, with his flashy clothes and abundance of gold jewellery, set her teeth on edge too. As did the way he looked at her, as if he was mentally stripping her.

Oh, well, she thought with a mental shrug. The evening won't last forever. It will just seem like it.

The club at the Zycos Regina impressed her immediately with its understated elegance, and subdued lighting. The clientele, mostly couples expensively dressed, were seated at tables set round an oval dance floor, and, on a corner dais, a quartet was playing soft dance music interspersed with interesting jazz.

'It's not very lively,' Lisa complained loudly, twisting round in her chair to survey the other patrons. 'If they're all so rich, why aren't they happier?'

Kate, uncomfortably aware of raised eyebrows and disapproving glances from adjoining tables, winced as she took a sip from the lurid cocktail that had been served to them all by an impassive waiter, and thought how much she'd have preferred a glass of wine.

It embarrassed her to see Dimitris flourishing a wallet full of notes, and clearly believing an extravagant tip allowed him to treat the staff like dirt.

It crucified her too to see Stavros stroking Lisa's exposed skin with a proprietorial hand and leering into her cleavage, then finding Dimitris leaning towards her, murmuring throatily with a suggestive smile, and reaching for her hand.

Deliberately, Kate edged her own chair away, feeling as if she'd woken to find herself in the middle of her worst nightmare.

We don't belong here she thought, with a sigh, as she began to plan her own strategic withdrawal. And we'd better leave before they ask us to go.

She wasn't sure of the moment when she knew she was being watched, but she felt the impact of the glance like a hand on her shoulder.

She drank some more of the unpleasant cocktail, then risked a swift look round, wondering resignedly if the management had already been summoned.

It was a corner table, set slightly apart from the others, and occupied by three men.

And the man watching her sat in the middle. In his early thirties, he was clearly younger than the other two, and, equally obviously, he was the one in control.

Even that first lightning assessment told her that he was good-looking, although not classically handsome. The dark face was strong, the lines of nose and jaw arrogantly marked. But more than that he exuded power, a charismatic force that could reach across a crowded room and touch its object like the caress of a hand.

She knew she should look away, but it was already too late. For an electrifying moment their eyes met, and locked, and Kate felt her breathing quicken and her throat tighten in an odd excitement.

But there was no warmth in his gaze. His expression was cool and watchful, his brows drawn together in a slight frown, as if something had displeased him.

And no prizes for guessing what that was, Kate thought, as she turned back to her companions, her face hot with embarrassed colour.

'Who's that?' Lisa had noticed the direction of her gaze, and was staring herself with open interest. 'Do you know him?' She giggled. 'Have you been holding out on me, Katie?'

'Not in the least,' Kate said crisply. 'Nor do I want to know him. I think he feels we're lowering the tone of the establishment.'

The fact that she thought exactly the same herself seemed paradoxically to increase her resentment.

'But I know him.' Stavros leaned forward, eyes gleaming. 'That is Michalis Theodakis. His father owns the whole Regina chain of hotels, and a great deal more, but the son now runs the company.'

Kate's brows lifted. 'Really?' she asked sceptically. 'What's he doing here?'

'He visits all the hotels,' Stavros explained. 'Checking them at random.'

'So who are the guys with him?' Lisa questioned.

'Who knows?' His minders probably.' His tone was envious. 'He is already a multi-millionaire in his own right, but he will be even richer when he gets control of all the Theodakis holdings. If he ever does,' he added, grinning.

'They say he and his father have quarrelled and Aristotle Theodakis would do anything to prevent him stepping into his shoes.'

He sent Kate a sly glance. 'Do you want him, *kougla mou*? Many women do, and not just for his money. He is quite a stud. You would have to stand in a long line, I think.'

'Don't be absurd,' Kate said coldly, aware that her flush had deepened. 'And do keep your voice down. I think he's planning to have us thrown out.'

That icy considering look had thrown her badly. He had seen her companions and judged her accordingly, so naturally she was honour bound to prove to him that his low opinion of her was entirely justified.

Teeth gritted, she reached for her drink, only to find the whole nasty concoction cascading down the front of her dress as her arm was jogged by a passing waiter.

She gasped and jumped up, shaking her skirt. Stavros and Dimitris were on their feet too, shouting angrily and gesticulating at the waiter, who was apologising abjectly and proffering a clean napkin.

'I'd better go to the powder room,' Kate interrupted, embarrassed at the attention the accident was attracting.

She turned, and cannoned into a tall figure standing behind her. As his hands grasped her arms to steady her, she realised it was Michael Theodakis.

'Allow me to make amends for the clumsiness of my staff, *thespinis*.' He spoke excellent English, she thought, with just a trace of an accent which, allied to his low-pitched drawl, some women would undoubtedly find sexy. 'If you will come with me, my housekeeper will attend to your dress.'

'There's really no need.' She freed herself, and took a small step backwards, her face warming. Because, close to, he was formidably attractive—over six feet in height, broad shouldered and lean-hipped. And prudence suggested she should keep her distance.

'But I think there is.' Somehow, he had repossessed her

hand, and was leading her between the tables towards the exit.

'Will you let go of me, please?' Kate tried to tug her fingers from his grasp. 'I can look after myself.'

'You are deluding yourself, *thespinis*, especially when you keep company like that,' he added with a touch of grimness.

She lifted her chin. 'It's not for you, *kyrie*, to criticise my friends.'

'They are old and dear acquaintances perhaps?' The sardonic note in his voice was not lost on her.

She bit her lip. 'Not—exactly.'

'I thought not.' He walked her across the hotel foyer to the row of lifts and pressed a button.

'Where are we going?' she asked in alarm, as the lift doors opened.

'To my suite.' He steered her inexorably inside. 'My housekeeper will join us there.'

'Take me back to the ground floor, please.' Kate was shaking suddenly. 'I want to go home—now.'

'It will be safer for you to remain at the hotel tonight.' He paused. 'I have a confession to make to you, *thespinis*. I sent Takis to spill your drink deliberately.'

'You must be crazy.' Kate felt dizzy suddenly. 'You can't hope to get away with this—even if you do own the place.'

'Ah,' he said softly. 'So you know who I am.'

'Your fame goes before you. But I'm not interested in being added to your list of conquests.'

He laughed. 'You flatter yourself, my red-headed vixen. My motives, for once, are purely altruistic.'

The lift doors opened, and Kate found herself being marched along a wide corridor towards a pair of double doors at the end.

'No.' There was real panic in her voice. 'I want to go home.'

'So you shall,' he said. 'In the morning when I am sure you have suffered no lasting ill effects.'

'Ill effects?' Kate echoed, as another wave of dizziness assailed her. 'What are you talking about.'

He said flatly, 'Your drink was spiked, *thespinis*. I saw your companion do it.'

'Spiked,' Kate repeated. 'You mean—drugged? But—why?'

He shrugged. 'To make you more amenable, perhaps.' He opened the door, and guided her into the room beyond. 'There is something called the date-rape drug. You may have heard of it.'

She said numbly, 'Heard of it—yes. But you must be mistaken. It can't be true…'

His mouth twisted. 'If the man you were with had asked you to sleep with him tonight, would you have agreed?'

She gasped. 'God—no. He's repulsive.'

'But might not take rejection well, all the same,' he said drily. 'Which is why you must not return to your apartment tonight.'

'But I have to.' Kate was shaking. She put a hand to her forehead, trying to steady herself. Collect her thoughts. 'My—my things are there. I'm going back to England tomorrow. Besides, they may have drugged Lisa too.'

His mouth curled. 'I doubt they would need to.'

She said hotly, 'You have no right to say that. You don't know her.'

He smiled faintly, 'I admire your loyalty, *thespinis*, if not your judgement. Now, I think you should lie down before you fall down,' he added with a slight frown.

'I'm—fine,' Kate said thickly.

'I don't think so,' he said, and picked her up in his arms.

She knew she should protest—that she should kick and fight, but it was so much easier to rest her head against his shoulder and close her eyes, and let him carry her.

She could feel the warmth of his body through his clothing. Could smell the faint muskiness of some cologne he wore.

She sensed a blur of shaded light, and felt the softness of a mattress beneath her. Dimly she was aware of her zip being unfastened and her dress removed, and tried to struggle—to utter some panicked negation.

A woman's voice spoke soothingly. 'Rest easily, little one. All will be well.'

Kate felt the caress of clean, crisp linen against her bare skin, and then the last vestiges of reality slid away, and she slept.

She dreamed fitfully, in brief wild snatches, her body twisting away from the image of Dimitris bending towards her with hot eyes and greedy hands, her voice crying out in soundless horror.

Once, there seemed to be a man's voice speaking right above her in Greek. 'She could solve your immediate problem.'

And heard a cool drawl that she seemed to recognise in the wry response, 'And create a hundred more...'

She wondered who they were—what they were talking about? But it was all too much effort when she was tired—so tired.

And, as she drifted away again, she felt a hand gently touch her hair, and stroke her cheek.

And smiled in her sleep.

CHAPTER THREE

SHE was on fire, burning endlessly in feverish, impossible excitement. Because a man's hands were touching her, arousing her to feverish, rapturous delight. His mouth was exploring her, his body moving against her as she lay beneath him, making her moan and writhe in helpless pleasure. In a need she had not known existed—until then.

And she forced open her heavy lids and looked at the dark face, fierce and intense above her, and saw that it was Michael Theodakis.

Kate awoke, gasping. For a moment she lay still, totally disorientated, then she propped herself up on an unsteady elbow, and looked around her.

Her first shocked realisation was that she was naked in this wide, luxurious bed, her sole covering a sheet tangled round her sweat-slicked body.

In fact, the entire bed looked as if it had been hit by an earthquake, the blue and ivory embroidered coverlet kicked to an untidy heap at its foot, and pillows on the floor.

It was a very large room, she thought, staring round her, with a cream tiled floor, and walls washed in a blue that reflected the azure of the sea and sky. The tall shutters had been opened, and the glass doors beyond stood slightly ajar, allowing a faint breeze from the sea to infiltrate the room and stir the pale voile drapes in the brilliant sunlight.

She shook the sheet loose, restoring it to a more decorous level, as she began slowly to remember the events of the previous night.

She didn't know which was the most extraordinary—the danger she'd been in, or the fact that Michael Theodakis had come to her rescue.

He must, she thought, have been watching very closely to have noticed her drink being spiked. But his attention would have been attracted by Stavros whom he'd clearly identified as trouble.

And he'd naturally be anxious to avoid any whiff of scandal being attached to his hotel, however marginal that might be. But whatever his motivation, she couldn't deny she'd had a lucky escape.

Shuddering, Kate sat up, shaking the tangle of red hair back from her face in an effort to dispel the faint muzziness which still plagued her—and paused, her attention suddenly, alarmingly arrested.

Because this room bore signs of occupation which had nothing to do with her, she realised, her heart thumping. Like a brush and comb and toiletries on the mirrored dressing table, a leather travel bag standing on a trestle in one corner, and a man's jacket tossed on to one of the blue armchairs by the window. And she could have no doubt about the identity of their owner.

She whispered, 'Oh God,' and sank back against the pillows, her mouth dry, and her mind working overtime.

Just exactly what had happened during the night? she asked herself desperately. And to be precise, what had happened after Michael Theodakis had carried her up here in his arms? Carried her to his room. His bed.

Because that she did most certainly recall, even if the rest was just a jumble of confused impressions.

But that was the effect of the date-rape drug, she reminded herself. It rendered you insensible. And it was only some time afterwards, if at all, that you remembered what had been done to you. And while she'd been unconscious, any kind of advantage could have been taken of her, she thought, swallowing painfully against her tight throat muscles.

Was it possible that during the hours of darkness, her rescuer could have turned predator?

Slowly, reluctantly, she made herself remember her

dream—that shivering, frenzied erotic ravishment that had tormented her unconscious mind.

But had it really been a dream, she wondered, staring, horrified, at the disordered bed—or stark reality?

Surely she would know—there would be some physical sign—if her body had been subjected to that level of sensual possession.

Or would she? Was this deep, unfamiliar ache inside her induced by physical frustration—or a passionate satisfaction that was entirely new to her?

Kate realised with shock that she could not be sure. And that maybe she never would be, which was, somehow, infinitely worse.

Oh, dear God, she thought, in panic. I've got to get out of here.

But where were her clothes? she wondered, staring fruitlessly round the room. Apart from her shoes, left by the bed, they seemed to have vanished completely.

And, as she absorbed this, a door opened and Michael Theodakis walked in.

Kate grabbed frantically at the slipping sheet holding it against her breasts, as her shocked brain registered that he himself was wearing nothing more than a towel draped round his hips. The rest of him was smooth olive skin, and rippling muscles, and in spite of herself, she found the breath catching in her throat.

He halted, looking her over slowly, brows lifted and eyes brilliant with amusement. He said '*Kalimera*. So you're awake at last.'

She stared at him, her pulse rate growing crazy. A sick certainty welling up inside her.

She said hoarsely, 'What—what are you doing here?'

'Shaving,' he said. 'A habit I acquired in adolescence.' He nodded towards the room he'd just left. 'I am sorry that we have to share a bathroom, but now you have it to yourself.'

'Share?' she said. 'A bathroom?'

'This suite only has one.' He seemed totally at ease with the situation, and with his lack of clothing too. But undoubtedly he was used to displaying himself in front of women in a towel, or even without one.

Whereas she—she was strangling in this bloody sheet.

'Which does not matter when I am here alone, as I usually am,' he went on.

'But last night,' Kate said, her voice shaking. 'Was different.'

'Of course,' he said softly. 'Because you were here.' He paused. 'I have ordered breakfast to be served to us on the terrace. Would you like me to run a bath for you?'

'No,' she said. 'I think I've had enough personal services for one lifetime. Like being undressed and put to bed last night.'

'You could not do it for yourself.' He made it all sound so reasonable, she thought in helpless outrage. 'You were barely conscious, *pedhi mou.*'

'I'm aware of that,' Kate said between her teeth. 'And I am not your little one.'

He frowned slightly. 'You have had a shock,' he said. 'But it is over now, and you have come to no harm.'

'Perhaps I don't see it like that.' The sheet was slipping, and she hitched it up, anchoring it with her arms. A gesture that was not lost on him.

There was still laughter in his eyes, but that had been joined by another element. Something darker—more disturbing. Something she had glimpsed in those dark, heated hours in the night, but did not want to recognise again.

Yet, at the same time, she realised that she had to confront him—had to know. Had to...

'Then how do you see it?' The dark eyes moved over her in frank assessment. He was enjoying this, she thought, her anger mounting. 'Maybe we can reach a compromise.'

Kate drew a shaky breath. 'I'd prefer the truth. Did you come to this room during the night.'

'Yes. I came to check that you were all right. So did the housekeeper, and also the hotel doctor. It was quite a procession,' he added drily.

She swallowed. 'But you were also here alone.'

He frowned. 'I have said so.'

She touched her dry lips with her tongue.

'Did you—touch me?'

There was a silence. Then, 'Yes,' he said quietly. 'I did not mean you to know, but I could not resist. Your hair looked so beautiful spread across my pillow. I had this irresistible desire to feel it under my hand.'

She stared at him. 'And was that all—your only irresistible desire, Kyrios Theodakis?'

He sighed. 'There was a tear on your cheek. I brushed it away.'

'And then you left,' she said. 'Is that what I'm supposed to believe?'

The dark eyes narrowed. He said softly, 'What are you trying to say?'

Kate bit her lip. 'Where exactly did you spend the night, Mr Theodakis?'

'This is a suite, Kyria Dennison. There are two bedrooms. I slept in the second. And I slept well. I hope you did too,' he added courteously.

'No,' she said. 'I didn't. I had the strangest dreams.'

The dark eyes narrowed. 'The effect of the drug, perhaps.'

'Perhaps,' she said. 'But this was such a vivid dream. So realistic.'

'You are fortunate,' he drawled. 'I rarely remember mine.'

'I'd give a hell of a lot,' Kate said stormily, 'not to remember this one.'

'You interest me.' He was frowning again, his eyes fixed watchfully on her flushed face. 'You can describe it to me over breakfast.'

'I don't want any breakfast,' she hurled at him. 'And I certainly don't want to eat with you. Because I don't believe it was a dream at all—you unspeakable bastard. Any more than I believe you spent the night in another room.'

His brows lifted. 'You're saying this dream involved me in some way?'

He sounded politely interested, no more. But there was a new tension in the tall figure. A sudden electricity in the room.

'Yes, I am. I'm saying you—used me last night.'

'"Used",' Michael Theodakis said musingly. 'An interesting choice of word. Do you mean that we made love?'

Kate's voice shook. 'I said exactly what I meant. And you took a filthy advantage of me. Oh, you're so damned sure of yourself,' she went on recklessly. 'So convinced that you're the answer to any woman's prayer. I expect you thought I'd be honoured—if I ever remembered.'

'So let us test this memory of yours,' he said softly. 'Tell me, *agapi mou*, exactly what I did to you.'

She said defensively, 'I can't recall the actual details.'

'But was it good for you?' He sounded almost casual. 'You must remember that. For instance, did you come?'

Kate gasped, colour flooding her face. 'How dare you.'

'But I need to know. I would hate to think I had disappointed you in any way.' He walked slowly towards her. 'Perhaps I should—jog your memory a little.'

'Keep away from me.' Kate shrank back.

'But why?' There was danger in his voice. He bent lithely, retrieving one of the pillows from the floor. Tossing it on to the bed beside her. His smile did not reach his eyes as he looked at her. 'When we have already been so close—so intimate? And this time, my beautiful one, I will make sure that you do not forget—anything.'

His hand snaked out, hooking into the folds of linen tucked above her breasts, and tugging them free, uncovering her completely.

Kate gave a small wounded cry, and turned instinctively on to her side, curling into a ball, and sheltering her body with her hands from the arrogance of his gaze, as humiliated tears burned in her throat.

'Why so modest?' His tone lashed her. 'According to you, there is nothing that I have not already seen and enjoyed.'

'Please,' she managed, chokingly. 'Please—don't...'

'But I am an unspeakable bastard, *agapi mou*,' he said softly. 'So why should I listen?'

She couldn't think of a single reason, huddled there on his bed, her breath catching on a sob.

For a moment there was silence and a heart-stopping stillness, then he sighed harshly, and turned away. He picked up a towelling robe from a chair and tossed it down to her.

'Put this on,' he directed curtly. 'You will find it safer than a sheet.'

As she obeyed hurriedly, clumsily, he went on, 'As you have just discovered, I have a temper, *thespinis*, so do not provoke me again. I have never taken a woman in anger in my life,' he added grimly. 'I do not wish you to be the first.'

She wrapped herself in the robe, tying the sash with shaking fingers.

He came to the side of the bed and took her chin in his hands, forcing her to look up at him.

He said quietly, 'The mind can play strange tricks, *pedhi mou*. But I swear I did not share your bed last night. Because if I had done so, you would have remembered, believe me.'

For a fleeting moment, his hands cupped her breasts through the thickness of the robe, his touch burning against her skin, making her nipples harden in sudden, painful need.

She heard herself gasp, then she was free, and he had stepped back from her.

He said, 'I am going to dress. Then you will join me for breakfast.'

She found the remains of her voice. 'My—clothes...?'

'My housekeeper took them to be laundered—after she undressed you last night.' He allowed her to absorb that.

'They will be returned to you after you have eaten.' He paused. 'Shall we say half an hour?'

And left her, staring after him, her bottom lip caught painfully in her teeth.

As she slid down into the scented bubbles of the bath, Kate was almost tempted to go one stage further, and drown herself.

Since the moment she'd opened her eyes that morning, she'd behaved like a crazy woman. But now she was sane again, and hideously embarrassed to go with it.

Oh, God, what had possessed her to hurl those accusations at Michael Theodakis? she asked herself despairingly.

Well, she supposed it had been triggered by him strolling in, next door to naked, and behaving as if it was an ordinary occurrence. As it probably was to him, but not to her...

She stopped right there, her brows snapping together.

What on earth was she talking about? Working as a holiday rep she encountered men far more skimpily clad every day, and had never found it any kind of problem.

So, why had she over-reacted so ludicrously? It made no sense. She bit her lip, as the realisation dawned that it was nothing to do with the way he'd been dressed—or undressed, and never had been.

It was Michael Theodakis himself who'd rattled her—sent her spinning out of control.

From the moment she'd seen him, she'd been on edge, aware of him in a way that was totally outside her limited experience. She'd been on the defensive even before he'd addressed one word to her.

And the dream, she guessed miserably, had simply been a spin-off from being carried upstairs in his arms. Maybe some humiliating form of wish-fulfilment.

So, she'd behaved like an hysterical fool and, in turn, been treated pretty much with the contempt she deserved, she thought, wincing.

She should have stuck to Plan A and just left quietly. After all, she could always have rung the apartment and got Lisa to bring her a change of clothes.

Lisa...

Kate groaned aloud. Until that moment, she hadn't spared her flatmate a thought. And anything could have happened to her.

This, she thought forcefully, is not like me.

Overnight she seemed to have turned into a stranger—and a stranger she didn't like very much.

In spite of her red hair, she'd always been cool, level-headed Kate, and she wanted her old self back. Michael Theodakis might be a devastatingly attractive man with a powerful sexual charisma, but that did not mean she had to go to pieces when she was around him.

Polite, grateful and unreachable. That was the way to handle the next half hour. The only way.

And then she would be gone, not just from this hotel, but from Greece too, and she would never have to set eyes on him again.

She dried herself and reluctantly donned the towelling robe again, knotting the sash for extra insurance. It masked her from throat to ankle, but it didn't inspire the confidence her own clothes would have done, and she needed all the assurance she could get, she thought wretchedly.

She combed her hair with her fingers, and emerged reluctantly into the bedroom, steeling herself to walk to the windows.

Outside, a table had been laid, overlooking the sea. And here Michael Theodakis was waiting, leaning against the balustrade in the sunlight.

Kate drew a deep breath, stuck her hands in the pockets of the robe to hide the fact that they were trembling, and went out to join him.

He was wearing shorts, which showed off those endless legs, she observed waspishly, and a short-sleeved polo shirt, open at the throat and affording a glimpse of the shadowing of body hair she'd already had plenty of opportunity to observe.

He said quietly, '*Kalimera*—for the second time. Or shall we erase the events of the past hour, which do credit to neither of us, and pretend it is the first?'

'Yes.' Kate looked down at the tiled floor, aware that she was blushing. 'Maybe we should—do that.'

'At last,' he said. 'We agree on something.'

She hastily transferred her attention to the table, set with a jug of chilled fruit juice, a basket of crisp rolls, dishes of honey and dark cherry jam, a bowl of thick, creamy yoghurt, a platter of grapes, apricots and peaches, and a tall pot of coffee.

She forced a smile. 'It all looks—delicious.'

'Yes,' he said softly, a quiver of amusement in his voice. 'It does.'

She found she was trembling suddenly, hotly aware that he was still looking at her, and not the food.

'Please sit down,' he went on, and Kate moved round the table, choosing a chair that would be as far away from him as it was possible to get, without actually jumping off the terrace. And she might even try that if all else failed.

'I hope you found your bath soothing,' he said silkily, as he poured the juice into glasses, and handed her one.

'Yes,' Kate said. 'Thank you.'

'But perhaps a body massage might be even more relaxing,' he went on. 'If you would like one, you have only to ask.'

Kate thumped an inoffensive bread roll on to her plate.

'How kind of you,' she said grittily. 'But I'll pass.'

He smiled at her. 'It was not a personal offer, *thespinis*. We have an excellent masseuse at the health spa, who comes highly recommended. But it's your decision.'

Wrong-footed again, thought Kate, taking a gulp of fruit juice and wishing dispassionately that it was hemlock.

'Honey?' Michael Theodakis proffered the dish. 'It might sweeten your disposition,' he added casually.

'My disposition is fine.' Kate spooned some on to her plate. 'Perhaps you just bring out the worst in me, Kyrios Theodakis.'

'My name is Michael,' he said. 'Or Mick, if you prefer. Just as you are Kate, rather than Katharina.'

She put down her knife. 'How do you know my name?' she demanded huskily.

He shrugged. 'Your papers were in the purse you left in the club last night. I did not think your identity was a secret. Besides, the police needed to know.'

'The police.' She stared at him, lips parted in shock, eyes widening.

'Of course.' He sounded matter of fact. 'Your friend Stavros also had ecstasy tablets in his possession when he was searched. Both he and his cousin spent the night in jail. The first of many, I suspect.'

'And Lisa?' Kate asked, with distress. 'Oh, God, they didn't lock her up too, surely.'

'No,' he said. 'I arranged for her to have her freedom. But it is as well she is leaving Zycos today, and I doubt she will ever be permitted to return. She keeps bad company.'

'You—arranged?' Kate said with disbelief. She shook her head. 'How gratifying to have such power.'

'No,' he said, and gave her a cool smile. 'Merely useful sometimes.'

Kate ate some bread and honey, forcing it past her dry throat.

At last she said stiltedly, 'I must sound very ungracious, *kyrie*.' She took a breath. 'I—I have to be grateful, to you, naturally. You saved me from potential disaster, but, for the rest of it, I'm totally out of my depth here.' She shook her head. 'Drug dealers—jail—I've never experienced these things before. I don't know how to handle them.'

He said quite gently, 'You don't have to, *thespinis*. They

have been dealt with for you. Please do not allow them to cloud your memories of Zycos.' He picked up the silver pot. 'Coffee?'

But, as she took the cup from him with a subdued murmur of thanks, Kate knew that it would not be her brush with the horror of Dimitris that would return to haunt her in the days to come, but the thought of this man, and the smile in his dark eyes. The warmth of his body, and the remembered scent of his skin as she'd been carried in his arms.

And, even more disturbingly, that there wasn't a thing she could do about it.

It was not the easiest meal Kate had ever eaten.

The necessity to appear untroubled—to make light, social conversation without revealing her inner turmoil—was an un-looked-for struggle.

'The weather's still wonderful,' she said over-brightly, after a pause. 'But I suppose it can't last forever.'

'Very little does.' He was preparing a peach, his long fingers deft, but he looked across at her and smiled. 'Did you know that the sun turns your hair to fire?'

'I'm aware it's red,' Kate said, with something of a snap. 'You don't need to labour the point.'

'And you should learn to accept a compliment with more grace, *matia mou*,' he said drily. 'Make the most of the sun,' he added. 'Because it will rain soon.'

She looked up at the cloudless sky. 'How do you know?'

He shrugged. 'These are my islands. It is my business to know. And our autumns tend to be damp.'

'Are you from Zycos originally?'

'No.' There was a sudden curtness in his voice. 'I was born on Kefalonia, and my real home was always there.'

'But no longer?' She remembered Stavros mentioning a family dispute.

He was silent for a moment. Then, 'I travel a great deal.

I have no permanent base just now.' He paused again. 'And you?'

'I share a flat in London.'

He frowned. 'With this Lisa?' There was a sudden austerity in his voice.

'Oh, no,' Kate said hastily. 'We were colleagues here for the season, and it just seemed—convenient. My flatmate in London is called Sandy, and she's very different. She works as a researcher on a national newspaper.' She hesitated. 'I shall—miss her when I move.'

'You are planning to do so?' He sounded politely interested.

'Yes,' she said. She took a deep breath. 'Actually—I'm going to be married. Quite soon. So—you see—I have every reason to be grateful for what you did for me. And I do—thank you. Very much indeed.'

There was silence—a slow tingling silence that threatened to stretch into eternity. Expressionlessly, Michael Theodakis looked down at her ringless hands. Studied them. Returned to her face.

He said, 'You are very much in love?'

'Naturally.' Kate stiffened defensively.

'And is it also natural to enjoy erotic fantasies about another man—a stranger?'

Her mouth was suddenly very dry. 'My fiancé is the one who matters. I'm not interested in anyone else.'

'Truly?' he asked softly. 'I wonder.' He pushed back his chair and came round the table to her, pulling her up out of her seat. His arms went round her, pulling her close to his body. Then he bent his head and kissed her, slowly and very thoroughly, his enjoyment of her mouth unashamedly sensuous.

Time stilled. His tongue was slow fire against hers, the practised mouth teaching her things she'd never known she needed to learn. Suddenly, she couldn't breathe—or think.

When he released her at last, he was smiling.

He said, 'I think, *pedhi mou*, that you are fooling yourself.'

Kate took a step backwards. She brushed a shaky hand across her burning lips, her eyes sparking anger at him. Anger she could shelter behind. 'You're despicable,' she flung at him. 'You had no right to do that—no right at all.'

He shrugged an unperturbed shoulder. 'Why not? I am a single man. You are a single woman.'

'But I told you. I'm going to be married.'

'Yes,' he said. 'You did. Be sure to send me an invitation to the wedding. If it ever happens. Because if I was going to marry you, Katharina *mou*, I would make sure you only dreamed of me.'

He lifted her hand, and dropped a brief kiss on to its palm, then turned and walked away into the suite, and out of her life.

Leaving her standing there in the sunlight, looking after him, white-faced and totally defenceless.

CHAPTER FOUR

SHE had a lot to think about on the flight back to Britain.

But her priority was the deliberate, systematic banishment of Mick Theodakis from her mind. Because there was nothing to be gained from remembering the glinting amusement in his dark eyes, or the incredible feel of his mouth on hers. Nothing at all.

So, she made herself contemplate her immediate future instead, which, to her dismay, proved just as tricky.

Because she knew with total and shattering certainty that she couldn't marry Grant. Not any more.

Clearly, he would want to know why she'd changed her mind, she thought wretchedly, and she didn't have a single reason to give that made any real sense, even to herself.

And whatever she said would be bound to hurt him, she thought wincing, and she didn't want to do that. Perhaps she could say that her time in Greece had changed her in some basic way. That she wasn't the same person any longer.

After all, it was no more than the truth.

But she had to recognise that she hadn't harboured a single doubt about her future with Grant until Michael Theodakis had crossed her path. Which was crazy, because you didn't overturn your entire life because of a casual kiss from a seasoned womaniser.

She needed to remember that, for Mick Theodakis, the kiss had been little more than a reflex action, she thought, plus an element of punishment for misjudging him.

All this she knew. So, why didn't it make any real difference?

She was still wondering when she walked into Arrivals

and saw Grant waiting for her, smiling, with a bouquet of flowers.

Kate's heart sank. She'd been counting on a slight breathing space before they met.

'Darling.' His arms hugged her close. 'God, I've missed you. From now on, I don't let you out of my sight. We have a wedding to plan, and I can't wait.'

She walked beside him in silence to the car, wondering how to begin.

'So, where's the crazy Lisa?' Grant asked cheerfully, as he stowed her bags in the boot. 'I thought she'd be with you.'

Kate bit her lip, remembering how she'd returned to the apartment to find it bare and empty, with Lisa's keys discarded on the living room table.

She said quietly, 'She decided to take another flight.' She took a deep breath, knowing she couldn't pretend—or hedge any more. 'Grant—I have something to tell you.'

His reaction was every bit as bad as she'd feared. He started with frank disbelief, moved to bewilderment, then to resentment and real anger.

On the whole, she thought, standing outside her flat, watching him drive away, the anger had been the easiest to cope with.

And now she had to deal with Sandy.

'Where's Grant?' was her flatmate's first inevitable question, after a welcoming hug. 'I was going to open a bottle of wine, then tactfully vanish.'

'No need.' Kate squared her shoulders. 'Grant and I are no longer an item.'

Sandy stared at her. 'When did this happen?'

'At the airport. He was making plans. I realised I couldn't let him.'

'Fair enough,' Sandy said equably. 'So—who's the new man?'

'Grant asked that too,' Kate said, aware that she was flushing. 'Why should my breaking up with him imply there's someone else?'

'Because that's the way it generally works.' Sandy poured the wine. 'So don't tell me he doesn't exist.'

Kate paused. 'It was nothing.'

'Then you did meet someone,' Sandy said triumphantly. 'I knew it.'

'No,' Kate shook her head. 'I *encountered* someone. Very briefly. Big difference.'

'Details please?'

'His name was Theodakis,' Kate said reluctantly. 'His family owns the Regina hotel chain, plus the Odyssey cruise fleet, and the Helicon airline. Does that tell you enough?'

'Absolutely.' Sandy gave her a narrow-eyed look. 'And that's a hell of a lot of info for just a brief encounter.'

'He didn't tell me all of it.' Kate's flush deepened. 'I—looked him up on the office computer before I went to the airport.'

'Good move.' Sandy approved. 'When's the wedding, and please may I be bridesmaid? I'd like to meet his friends.'

'I doubt he has any,' Kate said with a snap. 'He's arrogant and totally impossible.'

'Yet he's made you think twice about Grant, who's always been the soul of sweet reason.' Sandy clicked her tongue. 'I spy muddled thinking here, babe.'

'Not at all,' Kate retorted with dignity. 'I simply found out that absence—hadn't made my heart grow fonder.'

'Ah,' said Sandy. 'In that case, you should have no problem getting over Mr Theodakis either.' She raised her glass. 'Good luck,' she added cheerfully. 'You're going to need it.'

When Kate reported for duty at Halcyon's head offices a couple of days later, she was aware of an atmosphere, and sideways looks from other members of staff.

It didn't take her long to discover that Lisa had been fired, and had openly blamed Kate for getting her into trouble with the Greek police.

When the other girl came in to collect some paperwork, Kate confronted her, but Lisa remained obdurate.

'You dropped us all in it,' she accused. 'Now the lads are in jail, and I've got a police record. I'll probably never work in Greece again.'

'Lisa,' Kate said quietly. 'Stavros and Dimitris spiked my drink. They were seen doing it.'

'Rubbish,' Lisa said defiantly. 'It was just a giggle—something to relax you, and take the starch out of your knickers. You—over-reacted.'

'They were also carrying ecstasy tablets.' Kate spread her hands. 'They were drug dealers, Lisa. They could have caused us more trouble than we've ever dreamed of.'

Lisa shrugged, her face hard. She said, 'A word of advice. Whatever you may think of Stavros and Dimitris, they aren't even in the same league as Mick Theodakis. When it comes to ruthless, he invented the word. I don't know why he chose to meddle, but he probably had his own devious reasons. Because Sir Galahad he ain't.'

Kate bit her lip. 'Thanks—but I never thought he was.'

The next two weeks were difficult ones, especially when Grant decided to launch a charm offensive to win her back, turning up at the flat in the evening with flowers, bottles of wine, theatre tickets and invitations to dinner, all of which she steadfastly refused.

Work helped. Halcyon's winter City Breaks programme took her away a lot and, when she was at home, she let the answering machine field Grant's increasingly plaintive calls.

And eventually, her life steadied and found a new rhythm. A new purpose. One which did not include any lingering memories of Michael Theodakis, she told herself determinedly. And certainly no regrets.

After a weekend trip to Rome which had thrown up more than its fair share of problems, she was spending a wet

November afternoon at the office, working on a detailed report, when reception buzzed to say she had a visitor.

Kate groaned inwardly. Surely not Grant, again, she thought glumly as she rode down in the lift. He was beginning to be a nuisance, and she'd have to instruct Debbie to say she wasn't there in future.

She was already rehearsing the words, 'This has got to stop,' when the lift doors opened, and she stepped out into the foyer, to be brought up short, the blood draining from her face as she saw exactly who awaited her.

'Katharina,' Michael Theodakis said softly. 'It is good to see you again.'

Goodness, Kate thought breathlessly, has nothing to do with it.

He was lounging against the desk, immaculate in a formal suit and dark overcoat. Dressed for the City, for meetings and high-powered business deals. Smooth, she thought. Civilised. But she wasn't fooled for a moment.

She felt as if she'd strayed into a pet shop, and found a tiger on the loose.

Her mouth was suddenly dry. 'Mr Theodakis—what are you doing here?'

'I came to find you *matia mou*. What else?' He smiled at her, totally at his ease, the dark eyes making an unhurried assessment of her.

Making her feel, in spite of her neat grey flannel skirt and matching wool shirt, curiously undressed.

She said, her voice barely a whisper. 'I don't understand…'

'Then I will explain.' He straightened. The tiger, she thought, about to leap.

'Get your coat,' he directed. 'I have a car waiting.'

'But I'm working,' Kate said, desperately searching for a lifeline. 'I can't just—leave.'

'Mr Harris says you can, Miss Dennison.' Debbie, who'd been devouring him shamelessly with her gaze, broke in eagerly. 'Mr Theodakis spoke to him just now. I put him through,' she added proudly.

'Oh,' Kate said in a hollow voice. 'I see.'

One mention of the Theodakis name, she knew, would be enough to get the Halcyon boss jumping through hoops. He would dearly love to get exclusive rights at the Regina hotels for his holidays. And, quite suddenly, Kate had become the possible means to that end. Or so he would think.

In the cloakroom, Kate thrust her arms clumsily into the sleeves of her raincoat, but did not attempt to fasten it because her hands were shaking too much. When she tried to renew her lipstick, she ended up dropping the tube into the washbasin. Better not try again, she thought as she retrieved it, or she'd end up looking like a clown.

And she felt quite stupid enough already.

She found herself avoiding Debbie's envious glance as Michael Theodakis took her arm and walked her through the glass doors to the street.

The car was at the kerb, with a chauffeur waiting deferentially to open the door.

What else? Kate thought, as she sank into the luxury of the leather seating. And either I've gone crazy, or this is a dream, and presently I'll be awake again.

But there was nothing remotely dream-like about the man sitting beside her in the back of this limousine. He was living, breathing flesh and blood, and her every nerve-ending was tingling in acknowledgement of this. In terrifying awareness.

As the car drew away, he said, 'You are trembling. Why?'

No point in denial, she realised. He saw too much.

She said, 'I think I'm in shock.' She made herself look at him, meet the lurking laughter in his dark eyes. 'You're the last person in the world I ever expected to see again.'

He grinned at her, the lean body relaxed and graceful. 'Truly? Or did you just hope that I was out of your life?'

Kate lifted her chin. 'That too.'

'Then I am sorry to disappoint you,' he said without any

sign of contrition. 'But it was inevitable. The world is such a small place, Katharina *mou*. I always knew we would meet again. And I decided it should be sooner rather than later.'

Kate sat bolt upright. 'I can't think why.'

'Naturally, I wished to make sure you had recovered from your traumatic experience on Zycos,' he said silkily. 'Have you?'

'I never give it a thought,' Kate said shortly, resisting the urge to ask which particular trauma he was referring to.

'You are blessed with a convenient memory, *matia mou*.' His tone was dry. He looked her over, his glance lingering on the thrust of her breasts under the thin wool. 'You have lost weight a little. Why?'

'I lead a busy life.' His scrutiny brought a faint flush to her cheeks.

'Then you should make time to relax,' he said. 'Taste the wine. Feel the sun on your face.'

Kate sent a dry look towards the drenched streets. 'Not much chance of that today.'

'There is always sun somewhere, *agapi mou*.' He spoke softly. 'You must learn to follow it.'

'Then why aren't you doing so?'

'Because I am here—with you.' He paused. 'It is too early for dinner, so I thought we would go somewhere for tea. I told my driver the Ritz, but perhaps you'd prefer somewhere else.'

'That would be fine, although I can't imagine you'll find afternoon tea very exciting.' Kate tried to speak lightly.

He said gently, 'But you have yet to learn what excites me, Katharina.'

Kate's throat tightened. She felt herself blushing again, and bent her head slightly. A strand of hair fell across her cheek and she lifted a hand to brush it back.

He said, 'Leave it. You should not wear your hair scraped back from your face.'

'It's neat,' she said. 'And tidy. For work.'

'But you are not working now. And I like to see your hair loose on your shoulders. Or across a pillow,' he added softly.

Her face burned. 'But I don't style it to please you, Kyrios Theodakis.'

He smiled at her. 'Not yet, anyway.'

Kate tucked the errant tress behind her ear with a certain stony emphasis.

Immediately, she felt the focus of his attention shift. He moved sharply, his fingers closing round her wrists, capturing her hands while he studied them.

Kate tried to pull away. 'What are you doing?'

'Still no ring, *agapi mou*?' There was an odd note in his voice. 'Your lover cannot be very ardent. He should tell the whole world that you belong to him.'

Kate looked down at her lap. 'I—we decided to wait a little longer. That's all.'

His tone hardened. 'Katharina—look at me.'

Reluctantly, she obeyed, almost flinching at the sudden intensity of his gaze.

'Now,' he said. 'Tell me the truth. Are you engaged to this man? Do you plan to be married?'

She knew what she should do. She should tell him it was none of his damned business, and request him to stop the car and let her out.

The silence seemed to close round them. The air was suddenly heavy. Charged.

Kate swallowed helplessly. She heard herself say, 'I—I'm not seeing him. It's over.'

'Ah,' he said softly. 'Then that changes everything. Does it not, *agapi mou*?' Still watching the bewildered play of colour in her face, he lifted one hand, and then the other to his lips.

At the brush of his mouth, she found herself pierced by such an agony of need that she had to bite down on her lip to stop herself crying out.

Her voice shook. 'No. *Kyrie*—please...'

He made no attempt to release her. The dark eyes glittered at her. 'Say my name.'

'Mr Theodakis...'

'No.' His voice was urgent. 'Say my name as I wish to hear it. As you, in your heart, want to speak it. Say it now.'

Her mouth trembled. 'Michalis—*mou*.'

'At last you admit it.' There was a note of shaken laughter under the words. 'And now I will tell you why I am here. Because there is still unfinished business between us. I know it, and so do you.' He paused. 'Is it not so?'

'Yes.' Her voice was barely audible.

He made a slight, unsmiling inclination of his head, then leaned across and tapped imperatively on the driver's glass partition.

He said. 'The Royal Empress Hotel. And hurry.'

They stood together in the lift as it sped upwards. They were silent, but Kate could hear the sound of her own breathing, harsh, even erratic.

They did not touch, but every inch of her was quivering as if it already knew the caress of his hand.

Her heart was thudding painfully, as he unlocked the door, and ushered her into the large sitting room beyond.

Mutely, Kate allowed herself to be divested of her raincoat, then stood, trying to compose herself as she took stock of her surroundings.

It was a beautiful room, she saw, with elegant, highly polished furniture and large pastel sofas, complementing an exquisite washed Chinese carpet.

One wall seemed to be all glass, giving a panoramic view of the Thames.

And a door standing ajar allowed a glimpse of the bedroom with its king-size bed draped in oyster satin. Bringing her suddenly, joltingly back to a reality.

Dry-mouthed, she thought, 'What am I doing here?'

She knew she was being ridiculous. She was a grown

woman, and she was here of her own free will, but she was still as nervous as a teenager on her first date.

Because the truth was that she didn't really know what to expect. Not this time.

She'd been alone with Grant often, she reminded herself with a kind of desperation, either at her place or his, but she'd never felt like this. Never been so much at a loss, or in this kind of emotional turmoil.

But then her relationship with Grant had been quite different. They'd been finding out slowly and cautiously whether they might have a future together.

But, if she was honest, she'd never burned for him. Craved the touch of his mouth—the caress of his hands on her body. Never been so conscious of his sheer physical presence. She'd assumed that going to bed with Grant would be the final confirmation of their commitment to each other. Settled, even comfortable.

But with Michael Theodakis she could make none of those assumptions.

He would demand total surrender, and the thought of losing control of her body—and her emotions—so completely frankly terrified her.

But that wasn't all.

The brutal reality of the situation was that she'd come here to go to bed with a man she hardly knew. Someone infinitely more experienced than she was, who might well make demands she could not fulfil.

Biting her lip, she took a quick look over her shoulder.

He'd discarded his overcoat and jacket and was on the phone, waistcoat unbuttoned, tugging at his tie with impatient fingers as he talked.

She wandered across to the rainwashed window, and stared out, her thoughts going crazy.

If she told him she'd changed her mind, how would he react? she wondered apprehensively. He'd warned her that he had a temper. Could she risk provoking him again?

He replaced the receiver and came over to her, sliding his arms round her waist and drawing her back to lean against him. He bent his head, putting his lips against the side of her neck where the tiny pulse thundered.

He said softly, 'I hope you like champagne. I've asked them to send some up.'

'Yes,' she said breathlessly. 'That would be—lovely.' She glanced back at the window. 'On a fine day, this view should be spectacular.'

Oh, God, she thought. She was actually making conversation about the weather.

'Then it's fortunate it is raining.' He sounded amused. 'So we do not have to waste time admiring it.'

He turned her to face him, his hand sliding under the edge of her shirt to find the delicate ridge of her spine. Making her shiver in nervous anticipation as his fingers splayed across the sensitive skin.

He pulled her intimately, dangerously close to him, forcing her to the awareness that he was already strongly, powerfully aroused.

She stood awkwardly in the circle of his arms, her heart thudding. She thought, 'I don't know what to do...'

He cupped her face in his hands, making her look up at him.

He said. 'You are shaking. What is there to frighten you?'

She tried to smile. 'There's—you.'

His mouth twisted wryly. 'I am only a man, Katharina *mou*, not a monster. And I ask nothing that you have not given before.'

She said huskily, 'That's just the problem.'

He frowned slightly. 'I don't understand.'

She swallowed. 'Michael—I just don't—do things like this.'

His face was solemn, but his eyes were dancing. 'Is that a matter of principle, *agapi mou*, or do you simply not want to do them with me?'

She said baldly, 'I mean I never have.'

There was a pause. 'But you were seeing a man,' he said quietly. 'A man you planned to marry.'

'Yes,' she said. 'But we weren't—living together. We decided to—wait until I came back from Greece.'

He was very still. 'And before that?'

'There was no one I cared about sufficiently.' She stared rigidly at the pattern on his loosened tie. 'I—I always swore to myself that I'd avoid casual sex. That I'd only ever go to bed with a man if I couldn't help myself. If the alternative was altogether more than I could bear. I—I suppose I felt it should actually mean something...'

Her voice tailed off into silence.

'And now?' he asked.

She shook her head. 'I just don't—know any more.' She looked at him. 'I'm sorry. I should never have come here. I don't know what I was thinking of.' Her voice rose a little. 'I mean, we're strangers, for God's sake.'

'Hardly strangers,' he reminded her, a note of laughter in his voice. 'After all, you have spent one night in my bed already.'

'Yes,' she said huskily. 'But that time I was alone. Now it would be—different.'

'Yes,' he said. 'It would.'

There was another silence, as he looked down at her, his eyes meditative. His thumb stroked her cheek, and moved rhythmically along the line of her jaw, and the curve of her throat above her collar. She caught her breath, her heart juddering frantically.

'You don't want me to touch you?' he asked gently.

'I—didn't say that.'

'Then you think I will be unkind—uncaring in bed? That I will not give you pleasure?'

He sounded completely matter of fact—as if he was asking whether she preferred classical music to jazz, she thought wildly.

She said shakily, 'It's—not that. I'm scared I won't know how to please you. That you'll be disappointed.' She paused. 'You've had so many other women.'

'But never you, *matia mou*,' he said. 'Never until this moment. And while I have been seen with a great many women, I have actually slept with very few of them. Perhaps I think it should mean something too,' he added drily.

'Then—why me?'

He swung her round, so that she could see herself reflected in the window. He pulled the clip from her hair, letting it tumble in a shining mass on her shoulders.

'Look at yourself.' His voice was oddly harsh. 'This is the picture of you that I have carried in my mind—in my heart all these weeks. That has tormented me by day and kept me from sleep at night. And now I want the reality of you, naked in my arms. But, if necessary, I am prepared to wait. Until you are ready.'

She said unevenly, 'And if you have to wait a long time?'

He shrugged. 'I can be patient. But, ultimately, I expect my patience to be rewarded.'

He turned her round to face him, his hands framing her face.

'Do you accept that, Katharina?' His eyes seemed to pierce her soul. 'Do you agree that one day—one night—when you cannot help yourself—you will come to me?'

'Yes.' Her voice was a thread of sound.

He smiled, and released her, stepping back.

He said quietly, 'Then it begins.'

CHAPTER FIVE

AND that was where it should also have ended, Kate told herself bitterly.

She should have taken advantage of the brief respite he'd offered, and vanished. After all, Halcyon owed her leave, and she could have gone anywhere. Stayed away until he'd tired of waiting, and gone back to Greece. And found someone else to act as his smokescreen.

Her hair was dry, so, wearily, she began to make preparations for the night, turning off the fire, extinguishing lights, rinsing her beaker in the kitchen.

She was tired, but her mind would not let her relax from this emotional treadmill.

Oh, she'd been so easy to deceive, she thought, staring into the darkness. So eager to believe anything that he told her—to accept all that he seemed to be offering.

And he'd been clever too, making her think that she was in control—that she was making the choice. When really he'd been playing her like some little fish on his line.

Starting with that first afternoon...

The champagne had arrived with a bowl of strawberries, and a plate of small almond biscuits.

Michael had beckoned to her. 'Come and drink some wine with me,' he invited. 'And let us talk.'

Kate walked reluctantly across the room and seated herself on one corner of the sofa he indicated while he occupied the other.

'Is this a safe distance?' he asked mockingly, as he handed her a flute of champagne. 'I am not sure of the rules in this situation.'

'I expect you usually write your own.' The champagne was exquisitely cool and refreshing in her dry mouth.

'In business, certainly.' His tone was silky. 'But not usually in pleasure.' He let her digest that, then picked a strawberry from the dish, dipped it in champagne, and held it out to her. 'Try this.'

Kate bit delicately at the fruit, feeling self-conscious. 'That's—delicious.'

'Yes.' He was watching her mouth, as he took the next bite himself. 'It is.'

Kate crossed her feet at the ankles, nervously smoothing her skirt over her knees. 'So what do you want to talk about?'

'It occurred to me that we might get to know each other a little better.' He drank some champagne. 'What do you think?'

She shrugged nervously. 'If you wish. What do you want to know?'

'Everything.' He offered her another champagne-soaked strawberry. 'Are your parents living?'

'No,' she said. 'They died five years ago. Their car—skidded on black ice, and hit a wall.'

His brows snapped together. He said quietly, 'I am sorry, *pedhi mou*. Does it still hurt you?'

'Not like it once did.' She shook her head. 'But it meant I had to grow up fast, and make my own life, which I've done. And now I have a job I like which allows me to travel.' She paused. 'Are you an only child too?'

'I was for twelve years, and then my sister Ismene was born. She was only six when our mother died.'

'Oh,' Kate put down her glass. 'That must have been terrible.'

'It wasn't easy, especially for Ismene, although my aunt Linda did her best to take my mother's place.' He paused. 'The Regina hotels were named after her.'

Kate was silent for a moment. Then, 'What's your sister like?'

He considered. 'Pretty—a little crazy—and talks too much.' He shrugged, his mouth slanting wickedly. 'A typical woman.'

'Oh.' Kate's hands clenched into fists of mock outrage, and he captured them deftly, laughing as he raised them to his lips, then turned them so that he could brush her soft palms with his mouth, swiftly and sensuously.

'And she falls in love all the time with the wrong men,' he added softly. 'Something you would never do, I'm sure, *matia mou*.'

No, Kate thought, her heart pounding. But I could come dangerously close...

She removed her hands from his grasp, and picked up her glass again. A fragile defence, but all that was available.

'What—kind of men.'

'While she was at school in Switzerland last year, we had to buy off her art master, and a ski instructor.'

Kate choked back a giggle. 'She sounds quite a girl.'

'You could say that,' Michael agreed drily. 'In the end, my father decided it would be safer to keep her at home on Kefalonia.'

She waited for him to say something more about his father, but instead he took the champagne from the ice bucket and refilled her glass.

'I wasn't going to have any more,' she protested. 'I'm going to be drunk.'

'I don't think so.' He smiled as he replaced the bottle. 'A little less uptight, perhaps,' he added, proffering another strawberry.

She had plenty to be uptight about, Kate thought, taking a distracted bite and watching him transfer the rest to his own mouth.

Somehow, imperceptibly, as they talked, he'd been moving closer to her. Now, his knee was almost brushing hers, and his arm was along the back of the sofa behind her. She could even catch the faint, expensive fragrance of the cologne he used, reminding her, all too potently, of the brief giddy moments she'd spent in his arms.

She felt his hand on her shoulder, gently stroking its curve, and jumped, splashing champagne on to her skirt.

Michael clicked his tongue reprovingly, and leaned forward, brushing the drops from the fabric, his fingers lingering on her stockinged knee.

He said softly, 'I do not think the mark will be permanent.'

But he was so wrong, Kate thought, her pulses leaping frantically. Because she could be scarred for life.

He kissed her cheek, his lips exploring the hollow beneath the high bone, then dropped a fugitive caress at the very corner of her mouth. He traced the line of her jaw with tiny kisses, before allowing his tongue to tease the delicate whorls inside her ear.

As her head sank, helpless, on to his shoulder, his lips brushed her temples, her forehead, her half-closed eyes.

Everywhere he touched her, her skin bloomed, irradiated with a delight—an urgency she had never known before. Her whole body was melting, liquid with desire.

But he didn't kiss her mouth, as she needed him to do so badly, and his hand only caressed her shoulder and arm through the thin wool, and not her eager breasts.

And she was longing to feel his hands—his mouth on her body. To know him naked against her.

How was it possible, she wondered dazedly, for him to touch her so little, yet make her want him so much?

'Michael.' Her voice was husky suddenly, pleading. 'This—isn't fair.'

She felt him smile against her hair. 'Are you speaking of love—or war, *matia mou*?'

'But you said you wouldn't...'

'I came a long way to see you, *agapi mou*. Do you grudge me this small taste of you?' He tugged at her earlobe gently with his teeth. 'After all, I am torturing no one but myself.'

'You know,' she whispered. 'You know that isn't true.'

She turned, pressing her mouth almost frantically to his, begging him wordlessly for the response she craved.

But he moved back a little, framing her face between his hands.

He said, 'I think, Katharina, it would be wise if I took you somewhere for dinner now. We need other people round us.'

'Why?' She stared at him.

'Because if we stay here, you may have too much champagne and I—I may succumb to temptation.' He got to his feet in one swift lithe movement, pulling her up with him.

His voice sank to a whisper, 'So let us behave well, *pedhi mou*—for tonight at least.'

As they rode down in the lift, she said, 'I'm not really dressed for going out to dinner. Can it be somewhere not too smart?'

'Of course. No problem.'

'Oh,' Kate said. 'You've just reminded me of something.'

'What is it.'

She frowned, trying to remember. 'That night on Zycos, you were in my room talking to another man. Something about problems—solving them or causing them. I can't quite recall...'

There was an odd silence, then he shrugged. 'You must have been dreaming again, *pedhi mou*.'

'But it seemed so real,' she protested.

'So did the other dreams you had that night,' he reminded her drily, sending warm colour into her face. He paused, his mouth hardening and his eyes suddenly remote. 'But always reality is waiting.'

She felt as if a cold hand had touched her. She said his name questioningly, and he looked back at her, his face relaxing.

'Come, my beautiful one.' He took her hand. 'Let us enjoy our own dream a little longer.'

He was warning me, Kate thought, tears running down her face in the darkness. Because that's all it ever was—all it ever could be—a dream, and I was a fool to believe in it. To believe in him.

But I did, and now I have to live with the consequences. And the memories. And I don't know if I can bear it...

Lack of sleep left her feeling jaded, and aware of a slight headache the following morning. Although that was probably the least of her troubles, she reminded herself wearily.

And her day proved just as tricky as she'd expected. The French youngsters hadn't the slightest interest in the Tower of London and, clearly, would have preferred playing computer games in some arcade. But, in a way, Kate was glad of the challenge. Because it stopped her from thinking.

But when she'd bidden a final 'au revoir' to her reluctant charges and their harassed supervisors, she was once again alone, with a decision to make, and nowhere to hide.

She would have to agree, she thought wearily, as she let herself into the flat. Let him see that no sacrifice was too great in her determination to end their marriage.

But first a hot shower, to remove the kinks of the day, she thought, peeling off her clothes and reaching for her gingham robe. And also to give her time to think how to phrase her acceptance of his outrageous terms in a way that would leave her a modicum of dignity.

Not easy, she told herself wryly, as she adjusted the temperature control of the water.

She was just unfastening her robe when her front door buzzer sounded. For a moment she stood still, staring into space, her mouth drying as she realised the probable identity of her visitor.

Michael couldn't wait for her answer, of course. Oh, no, he had to apply the pressure, she thought bitterly.

She could always pretend to be out, she told herself, then remembered that her living room light was on and clearly visible from the street. On the other hand, she didn't have to let him in.

She tightened the sash round her waist, then walked to the intercom panel by the door.

'Yes?' Her tone was curt.

'Darling,' Grant said. 'I need to see you. Please let me in.'

It was almost, but not quite, a relief to hear him.

She said, 'It's not really convenient...'

'Katie,' he interrupted firmly. 'This is important. We have to talk.'

Sighing, Kate released the front entrance button, and walked to her own door.

'I've been worried about you,' he said, as he came in. 'You haven't returned any of my calls.'

She sighed again, under her breath. 'Grant, when I came back from Greece you were very kind, and I'll always appreciate it, but we can't live in each other's pockets. But as I've tried to tell you, we both need to move on.'

'Darling, you need time. I understand that. But as for moving on...' He handed her the newspaper he was carrying. 'Have you seen this?'

It was a picture of Michael, leaving the airport, smiling, and a caption.

Millionaire tycoon Michael Theodakis flew in yesterday to finalise the acquisition of the ailing Royal Empress group for his Regina Hotel chain. He is also planning a romantic reunion with his English bride of eight months, Katharine, who has been spending a few weeks in London.

'Oh, God.' Kate's throat tightened uncontrollably, as she threw the paper to the floor. 'I don't believe this.'

'Talk to your lawyer,' Grant advised authoritatively. 'Get an injunction.'

She wrapped her arms round her shaking body. 'It's a little late for that. I've already seen him.'

Grant stared at her. 'But when you came back, you said it was over. That you were never going to see him again.'

'Mick has other ideas.' Kate drew a steadying breath. 'In fact, he's asked me to go back to Kefalonia with him for a family wedding. But it's no romantic reunion,' she added wearily, as Grant's mouth opened in protest. 'It's a *quid pro quo* arrangement. I do him this favour. He gives me a quick divorce.'

'Kate, for God's sake.' Grant's voice rose. 'Don't tell me you're actually considering this preposterous deal.'

'Oh, but she is,' Mick said softly from the doorway. 'If it is any concern of yours.'

He was leaning against the doorframe, apparently at his ease, but his eyes were like obsidian, and there was a small, cold smile playing about his mouth.

Kate swallowed. 'How—how did you get in?'

'Your obliging neighbour again.' His icy gaze scanned the gingham robe, then turned inimically on Grant. 'She did not realise you were already—entertaining.'

'I'm not,' Kate said angrily aware that her face had warmed. But what the hell did she have to feel guilty about? Mick was the one who'd betrayed her. Who'd destroyed their marriage.

She bent and retrieved the newspaper. 'Grant just came to bring me a message. He's—just leaving.'

'Kate,' Grant gasped.

She didn't look at him. 'Just go—please.'

'Very well.' He gave Mick a fulminating look as he stalked past him. 'But I shall be back.'

'No,' Mick said, his eyes flicking him with cool disdain. 'You will not.'

For a moment they faced each other, then Grant, his face working, turned away, and Kate heard him going down the stairs.

Mick walked forward into the room, and kicked the door

shut behind him. He said, 'Your guard dog lacks teeth, *pedhi mou.*'

'Grant is a friend, nothing more.' Kate faced him defiantly.

'You once thought you were in love with him,' he said. 'And now I find you here with him, half-naked.'

'I'm perfectly decent,' she flung at him. 'I was about to have a shower when he arrived.'

Mick took off his jacket and flung it across a chair. 'Did you plan to share it with him, as you used to do with me?' His voice was low and dangerous.

'And what if I did?' Her voice shook, not just with anger but pain. 'You have no right to question me—not with your track record, you—appalling hypocrite.'

'You think not? Maybe it is time I reminded you, *agapi mou*, that you are still my wife.'

He reached her in one stride. His hands grasped her arms, pulling her forward, and his mouth descended crushingly on hers. At first she fought him in sheer outrage, but he was too strong, and too determined, his fingers tangling in her hair, as his lips forced hers apart.

She couldn't breathe—she couldn't think. She could only—endure, as his hand swept her from breast to thigh in one stark act of possession. Reminding her with terrifying emphasis that her body's needs had only been suppressed. Not extinguished.

When at last he let her go, she took a shaky step backwards, stumbling over the hem of her robe in her haste, and pressing a hand to her reddened mouth.

'You bastard,' she choked. 'You bloody barbarian.'

'I am what I always was,' Mick retorted curtly. 'And I have warned you before not to make me angry.'

'You have no right to be angry. Or to accuse me when you—you...'

The words stuck in her throat. She couldn't speak them. Couldn't face him with his betrayal. Not then. Not now. It hurt too much, and always had. Besides, she might cry in front of him—the great agonised sobs which had torn her apart night after night when she'd first fled from Kefalonia. And she couldn't let him see what he had done to her—how close he'd brought her to the edge of despair and heartbreak.

By remaining silent, she could perhaps hang on to some element of her pride.

He shrugged. 'I'm a man, Katharina, not some plaster saint on an altar. I made no secret of it, yet you still married me.' His tone was dry.

'And very soon lived to regret it,' she flashed.

'Even with all that money to sweeten my barbaric ways,' he mocked her. 'You are hard to please, my Kate.'

She said in a low voice, 'I am not—your Kate.'

'The law says otherwise.'

'Until I get my decree.'

'For which you need my goodwill,' he said softly.

'I think the price may be too high.' She steadied herself, and looked back at him. 'I want it understood that my return to Kefalonia does not give you the right to—maul me whenever the whim takes you.'

'Not a touch, *agapi mou*?' His drawl mocked her. 'Not a kiss?'

'Nothing,' she said. 'Otherwise the deal's off—however long it takes me to be rid of you.'

'I'll settle for a pretence of affection, and some common civility, *matia mou*.' There was a harsh note in his voice. 'I'm told when you worked on Zycos, you were a model of diplomacy. Bring some of your professional skills to bear.'

Kate bit her lip. 'When exactly am I expected to begin this—charade?'

'At once.' He pointed to the crumpled newspaper she was still clutching. 'As you see, your tabloids have discovered that we are both in London, but not together. That must be remedied at once. I do not choose to have my private life examined by the gutter press.'

Kate stiffened. 'In what way—remedied?'

'By packing what you need, and coming with me to the hotel tonight. Making the resumption of our marriage public.'

'But we're getting a divorce,' she objected. 'You can hardly keep that a secret.'

'Let us deal with one problem at a time. Tonight, I require you to accompany me to the Royal Empress.'

'The Royal Empress.' The breath caught in her throat. 'No—I won't do it. I agreed to attend Ismene's wedding, but nothing was said about—cohabiting with you here in London.'

He said coldly, 'That is not for you to choose. Nor is it what I intended, or wished,' he added with cutting emphasis. 'However, it is—necessary, and that must be enough.' He paused. 'But I am using the penthouse suite—one that holds no memories for either of us.'

She looked down at the floor, swift colour rising in her face, angry that he should have read her thoughts so accurately. Angry, too, that she'd let him see she was still vulnerable to the past.

'It is larger too,' he went on. 'With luck, *matia mou*, we may never be obliged to meet. And certainly not—cohabit.'

Kate bit her lip. 'Very well,' she agreed, her voice constricted. She hesitated. 'I—I'll get my stuff together. Perhaps you'd send the car for me—in an hour.'

Mick sat down in her armchair, stretching long legs in front of him. He said, 'I can wait.'

'But I've got things to do,' she protested. 'I told you—I was going to have a shower.'

'Then do so.'

'There's no need to stay on guard,' she said. 'You surely don't think I'm going to do a runner?'

His mouth curled slightly. 'It would not be the first time, my dear wife. I am not prepared to take the risk again. Now, go and take your shower.'

Kate gave him a mutinous look, then went into her bedroom, and closed the door. She looked over the small stock of clothing in her wardrobe, most of it cheap casual stuff bearing no resemblance to the collection of expensive designer wear that she'd abandoned on Kefalonia.

But, then, she was no longer the same girl, she reminded herself.

She put underwear, a couple of cotton nightdresses and some simple pants and tops in to her travel bag. After her bath, her housecoat and toiletries would join them.

She collected fresh briefs and bra, and picked a knee-length denim skirt and a plain white shirt from her remaining selection of garments. Practical, she thought, but the opposite end of the spectrum from glamorous.

Carrying them over her arm, she trailed self-consciously from the bedroom to the bathroom.

Mick was reading her discarded newspaper.

'I hope you've forgotten nothing,' he said courteously, without raising his eyes.

'I hope so too.' Damn him, she thought. He never missed a trick.

And she didn't need him to point out, however obliquely, the contrast between the warm joyous intimacy of their early married life where no doors were ever closed, and the embarrassed bitter awkwardness of their present relationship. She was already well aware—and hurting.

'Would you like me to wash your back?' His voice followed her. It held faint amusement, and another intonation that sent a ripple of awareness shivering down her spine.

'No,' she said curtly and slammed the door on him, and the memories the question had evoked. She shot the bolt for good measure, although it was too flimsy to debar anyone who really wanted to come in.

She swallowed, firmly closing her mind against that possibility.

The warm water was comforting but she was not disposed to linger. Besides, commonsense told her that it would not be wise to keep Mick waiting too long, she thought wryly, as she dried herself swiftly and put on her clothes.

Armouring herself, she realised, as she brushed back her hair, and confined it at the nape of her neck with a silver clip. And if Mick didn't like it, he could lump it, because she was going to need every scrap of defence she could conjure up.

Drawing a deep breath, she slid back the bolt and emerged. She said, 'I'm ready.'

He was shrugging on his jacket, but he paused, looking her over with narrowed eyes in a lengthening silence.

'Are you making some kind of statement, Katharina?' His voice was gentle, but cold.

'I dress to please myself now.' Kate straightened her shoulders. 'I'm sorry if I don't meet your exacting standards.'

Mick sighed. 'Tomorrow, *pedhi mou*, I think you must pay a visit to Bond Street.'

She lifted her chin. 'No. And you can't make me.'

He gave her a thoughtful glance. 'Is this what you wear at your work?'

'Of course not. The company supplies a uniform.'

'But now you are working for me,' he said softly. 'In a different capacity. Which also requires a uniform. So, tomorrow you will go shopping. You understand?'

Looking down at the floor, she gave a reluctant nod.

'And you will also wear this.' He walked across to her, reaching into an inside pocket, and produced her wedding ring.

'Oh, no.' Instinctively, she put both hands behind her back. His name was engraved inside it, she thought wildly, and the words 'For ever.' She couldn't wear it. It was too cruel. Too potent a reminder of all her pitiful hopes and dreams.

She said, 'I—I can't. Please...'

'But you must.' He paused, his gaze absorbing her flushed cheeks and strained eyes, then moving down to the sudden hurry of her breasts under the thin shirt, his dark eyes narrowed, and oddly intent.

He lifted his hand and ran his thumb gently along the swell of her lower lip. He said in a low voice, 'I could always—persuade you, *agapi mou*. Is that what you want?'

A shiver tingled its way through her body. 'No.'

'Then give me your hand.'

Reluctantly, she yielded it. Watched, as he touched the gold circlet to his lips, then placed it on her finger. Just as he had done on their wedding day, she thought, as pain slashed at her. And if he smiled down into her eyes—reached for her to kiss her, she might well be lost.

But he stepped back, and there was the reassurance of space between them.

And, building inside her, anger at his hypocrisy—his betrayal.

She whispered, 'I hate you.'

There was a sudden stillness, then he gave a short laugh.

'Hate as much as you want, Katharina *mou*,' he said harshly. 'But you are still my wife, and will remain so until I choose to let you go. Perhaps you should remember that.'

As if, Kate thought, turning blindly away, as if I could ever forget.

CHAPTER SIX

THE journey to the hotel was a silent one. Kate sat huddled in her corner of the limousine, staring rigidly through the window, feigning an interest in the shop-lined streets, the busy bars and restaurants they were passing.

Anything, she thought shakily, that would reduce her awareness of the man beside her. And the unbridgeable gulf between them.

As the driver pulled up in front of the Royal Empress, she heard Mick swear softly under his breath.

He said quietly, 'Not a word, *matia mou*—do you hear me?'

Then, suddenly, shockingly, she was being jerked towards him. She felt the silver clip snapped from her hair, found herself crushed against him, breast to breast, held helplessly in his arms while his mouth took hers, hard, experienced and terrifyingly thorough.

Then the car door was open, and she was free, emerging dazedly on to the pavement, standing for a moment as cameras flashed, then walking pinned to Mick's side, his hand on her hip, to the hotel entrance.

'Quietly, my red-haired angel.' She heard the thread of laughter in the voice that whispered against her ear. 'Scream at me when we're alone.'

People were greeting her. She saw welcoming, deferential smiles, and heard herself respond, her voice husky and breathless.

The manager rode up in the lift with them, clearly anxious that his arrangements should be approved by his new employer.

It was a beautiful suite. Even anger and outrage couldn't

blind Kate to that. There was the usual big, luxuriously furnished sitting room, flanked on either side by two bedrooms,
each with its own bathroom.

There were flowers everywhere, she saw, plus bowls of
fruit, dishes of handmade chocolates, and the inevitable
champagne on ice. By the window was a table, covered in
an immaculate white cloth, and set with silverware and can-
dles for a dinner *à deux*.

All the trappings, Kate thought, her heart missing a beat,
of a second honeymoon...

Someone was carrying her single bag into one of the bedrooms with as much care as if it was a matching set of Louis
Vuitton, and she followed, hands clenched in the pockets of
her navy linen jacket.

One of the walls was almost all mirror and she caught a
glimpse of herself, her hair loose and tousled on her shoulders, her mouth pink and swollen from kissing, even a couple
of buttons open on her shirt.

She looked like a woman, she thought dazedly, whose man
couldn't keep his hands off her.

'We are alone.' Mick was standing in the doorway behind
her, his dark face challenging. 'So, you may shout as much
as you wish, *pedhi mou.*

She took a deep, breath. 'What the *hell* was all that about?'
Her voice shook.

He shrugged. 'I saw the cameras waiting for us. They
wanted proof that our marriage was solid. It seemed wise to
give it to them. I have my reasons,' he added coolly.

'Reasons?' she echoed incredulously. 'What possible reason could there be?' She tried to thrust her buttons back into
their holes with trembling fingers. 'You made it look as if
we'd been having sex in the back of the car.'

'No,' he said. 'The prelude to sex perhaps.'

'There's such a big difference.' Her voice radiated scorn.

He had the nerve to grin at her. 'Why, yes, *matia mou.* If

you remember, I prefer comfort—and privacy. I find the presence of a third person—inhibiting.'

But there was always someone else there, she thought in sudden agony, although I didn't realise it then. Every time we touched—made love, Victorine was there—Victorine...

She lifted her chin. 'I hope you haven't arranged any more—photo opportunities. Because I won't guarantee to co-operate.'

'Is that what you were doing in the car—co-operating?' Mick asked sardonically. 'I would never have guessed.'

She glared at him. 'I never pretended I could act.'

He said courteously, 'You do yourself less than justice, *pedhi mou*.' He glanced at his watch. 'At what time do you wish them to serve dinner?'

'I'm not hungry.'

Mick sighed. 'Would your appetite improve if I said that you were dining alone?' he asked wearily.

'Oh.' She was taken aback. 'You're going out?'

He shrugged. 'Why not?'

She bit her lip. 'I'll order something later—a club sandwich maybe.'

'The chef will be disappointed—but the choice is yours.'

She unfastened her travel bag. 'I think we both know that isn't true,' she said tautly. 'Or I wouldn't be here.'

She extracted her uniform dress and jacket, and moved towards the fitted wardrobes.

'What are those?' His tone sharpened.

'My work clothes.' Kate paused, hanger in hand.

'Why have you brought them?'

'Because I have a job to go to in the morning,' she said. 'But perhaps it's a trick question.'

'You had a job,' Mick corrected, the dark brows drawing together haughtily. 'If you write out your resignation, I will see it is delivered.'

Kate gasped. 'I can't do that. And I won't,' she added

stormily. 'When this—farce is over, I'm going to need a career.'

'But the farce has still a long time to run,' Mick said with steely softness. 'And in the meantime, Katharina *mou*, my wife does not work.'

'And how long does this embargo last?' Her voice shook. 'Until after the divorce?'

'Forever,' he said curtly. 'Married or divorced, I shall continue to support you financially. As I am sure your lawyer has made clear,' he added with a certain grimness.

'Yes,' Kate said raggedly. 'And I want nothing from you—except my freedom. You don't have to buy me off, *kyrie*, or pay for my silence, either.' She took a deep breath. 'Our marriage—should never have happened, but I won't dish the dirt on it—sell the unhappy details to the newspapers. And I'll sign any confidentiality clause that your legal team can dream up.'

He was very still. He said slowly, '"Unhappy details" *matia mou*? Is that—truly—all you remember?'

For a moment, her mind was a kaleidoscope throwing up image after image. Mick walking hand in hand with her through the snow in Central Park—teaching her to skate, both of them helpless with laughter—fetching paracetamol and rubbing her back when she had curse pains.

And holding her as she slept each night.

That above all, she thought with agony. The closeness of it. The feeling of total safety. Of what I thought was love...

She looked stonily back at him. She said, 'What else was there?'

He said with immense weariness, 'Then there is nothing more to be said.'

As he turned away, she said swiftly, 'Before you go—may I have my hairclip, please.'

'I'm sorry.' Face expressionless, he gave a brief shrug. 'I must have dropped it in the car—or in the street, perhaps. Is it important?'

'No,' she said slowly. 'It doesn't really matter.'

And watched him walk out, closing the door behind him.

'Nothing matters,' she whispered, when she was alone. 'Nor ever will again.' And felt tears, hot and thick in her throat.

She walked over to the wide bed, and sat down on its edge, burying her face in her hands.

Who was the first person, she wondered, to state that love was blind?

Because she'd realised that she'd fallen in love with Michael Theodakis before they'd even sat down to their first dinner together, loved him, and longed for him during the weeks that followed.

Every night that he'd been in London, and he seemed to be there a great deal, his car was waiting for her when she left work.

He took her to wonderful restaurants, to cinemas, theatres and to concerts. He took her for drives in the country, and walks in the park.

He did not, however, take her to bed.

His lovemaking was gentle, almost decorous. There were kisses and caresses, but the cool, clever hands that explored her body aroused, but never satisfied. He always drew back before the brink was reached, courteously, even ruefully, but with finality.

Leaving her stranded in some limbo of need and frustration, her senses screaming for fulfilment.

She was on wires, her eyes as big as a cat's, her face all cheekbones.

Only Sandy knew her well enough to be concerned—and to probe.

'Do you know what you're doing?' she asked abruptly one day, when Kate was trying on the little black dress she was planning to borrow from her.

'What do you mean?' Kate's tone was defensive.

Sandy sighed. 'You're swimming with a shark, love.' She sat down on the edge of the bed.

'I thought you liked Mick.' Kate stared at her distressed.

'I do like him. He's seriously good-looking, too charming for his own good, and filthy rich. What's not to like?'

Kate forced a smile. 'And I'm none of those things, so why is he bothering with me? Is that it?'

Sandy spread her hands. 'Kate, I'm in love with Gavin, and going to be married, but when Mick Theodakis does that smiling-with-his-eyes thing, I become a melted blob on the carpet. I can understand why you're seeing him.'

She paused. 'But honey, he's seen a lot of women. He's been on some "eligible bachelors of the world" list since he was in his teens.'

She shook her head. 'You know who he used to date? That supermodel who became an actress—Victorine. One of the girls on the social page told me that they were a real item. He was supposed to be crazy about her—talking marriage—the whole bit. Now, he's back on the market, and she's gone to ground somewhere, and no one's heard of her for over a year.'

She got to her feet. 'The thing is, he may not believe in long-term commitment, Katie, and I don't want you to break your heart.'

I think, Kate told herself wryly, that it may be a little late for that.

The following day Mick flew to New York and was there for about a week. He called several times, but, just the same, she missed him almost desperately.

On the day of his return, she flew out of the office, only to find a complete stranger waiting for her.

'Kyria Dennison?' He was a stocky man, with dark shrewd eyes, and a heavy black moustache, and she recognised him as one of the men sitting with Mick in the nightclub the night they met. 'I am Iorgos Vasso. Kyrios Michalis sends his apologies, and asks me to escort you to the hotel.'

'Is he ill?' Kate questioned anxiously.

The dark eyes twinkled. 'He is jet lagged, *kyria*. Sometimes it affects him more badly than others.'

'Oh,' Kate said slowly. 'Well—maybe I should leave him to rest.'

'Jet lag is bad,' Iorgos Vasso said solemnly. 'But disappointment would be far worse. Let me take you to him.'

'Your voice sounds familiar,' Kate said, frowning a little, as the car inched its way through the traffic. She paused. 'Didn't I hear you talking with Mr Theodakis in my room that night on Zycos—about solving a problem?'

He shrugged, his smile polite and regretful. 'Perhaps, *kyria*. I really don't remember.'

She sighed. 'It doesn't matter.'

Mick was waiting for her impatiently in the suite. He looked rough, but his smile made her heart sing. He pulled her into his arms and held her for a long time.

'This week has been hell,' he told her quietly. 'Next time, I take you with me.'

They dined quietly in the sitting room, but he only toyed with his food.

'I'm, exhausted, *pedhi mou*,' he told her frankly, when the meal had been cleared away. 'Would you mind if I took a nap for half an hour? I will try to be better company afterwards.'

'You're sure you don't want me to go—give you some peace?'

'No.' He kissed her. 'Wait for me—please.'

He went into the bedroom, and shut the door. When he still hadn't reappeared nearly two hours later, Kate went across and tapped on the door.

There was no reply, so, she turned the handle gently and peeped in. One shaded lamp burned in the room and Mick was lying on top of the bed, sound asleep, his shoes and jacket discarded.

Kate walked to the bed, and stood looking down at him.

She had never seen him sleeping before and, with his long eyelashes curling on his cheek, he looked much younger. Almost vulnerable.

He's not going to wake up, she thought. I could simply kiss him goodnight, and leave.

Instead, she found herself kicking off her own shoes, and lying down beside him on the satin coverlet.

She wasn't planning on sleeping herself. She just wanted to lie quietly for a while, and watch him, and listen to his soft, regular breathing.

But the room was warm, and the bed soft and comfortable, its crisp linen faintly scented with lavender and, in spite of herself, Kate found her eyelids drooping.

She thought, 'I ought to go home…' And then she stopped thinking altogether.

She awoke suddenly with a start, and looked around, momentarily disorientated, wondering where she was. Then she saw Mick, propped on one elbow, studying her, his face grave, his dark eyes hooded.

She said, a little breathlessly, 'I must have—fallen asleep. What time is it?'

'The middle of the night.' His brows lifted. 'You should be more careful, *matia mou*. Has no one told you it is dangerous to tempt a hungry man with crumbs?'

She said, with a catch in her voice, 'Perhaps I'm starving too.'

He smiled into her eyes, as he smoothed the dishevelled hair back from her face, and ran his finger gently across her parted lips.

He said softly, 'I hope it is true, yet you may still change your mind—if you wish.' He paused. 'But if you allow me to touch you, it will be too late.'

'I'm here because I want to be,' she whispered. 'Because I can't help myself.'

She sat up, and pulled off her black sweater, tossing it to the floor.

Mick drew a sharp breath, then took her into his arms, kissing her slowly and very deeply.

His hands were unhurried, too, as they removed the rest of her clothes, his lips paying sensuous homage to every curve and hollow that he uncovered.

When she was naked, he looked at her for a long moment. He said huskily. 'How beautiful you are.'

Shy colour burned in her face, but she met his gaze. 'You've seen me before.'

'But then you were angry.' His hand cupped her breast, his fingers teasing her nipple, making it stand proudly erect. 'You were not like this. So sweet—so willing.'

But when she tried to unbutton his shirt, to undress him in turn, he stopped her, his hands closing over hers.

'Not yet.' He kissed her again, his mouth warm and beguiling, then bent his head to her breast, his tongue flickering against the taut rosy peak. 'First, *agapi mou*,' he murmured, 'I need to pleasure you.'

It was a long, languorous journey into arousal. Kate found herself drifting almost mindlessly, aware only of the message of her senses in response to the whisper of his hands and mouth on her body. Conscious of the slow, irresistible heat building within her that demanded to be assuaged. Somehow.

When his hand parted her thighs, she heard herself make a small sound in her throat, pleading, almost animal.

'Yes.' His low voice seemed to reach her from some vast distance. 'Soon—my dove, my angel, I promise.'

His fingers explored her gently, making her gasp and writhe against his touch. Almost immediately it changed, his fingers still stroking her delicately, but creating a new, insistent rhythm as they did so. Gliding on her. Circling. Focusing on one small, exquisite point of pleasure.

Her body moved restlessly, searching, seeking, as her awakened senses whispered of a goal to be attained.

As his fingers strummed the tiny moist pinnacle of heated

flesh, his mouth enclosed her breast, caressing the sensitised peak with his tongue.

Delight lanced through her as she arched towards him in wordless demand.

It was difficult to breathe. Impossible to think. She could only—feel.

Then, deep inside her, she experienced the first sweet burning tremors that signalled her release. Felt them ripple outwards. Intensify. Heard herself sob aloud as the last vestiges of control fell away, and her entire being was consumed—ravished by pulsations so strong she thought she would be torn apart.

The storm of feeling lifted her, held her in a scalding limbo, then let her drift in a dizzying spiral back to earth.

She lay, dazed, trying to regulate her ragged breathing.

She was vaguely aware that Mick had moved slightly, shifting away from her, and she tried to murmur a protest from her dry throat.

He said softly, 'Rest a little, *pedhi mou*.' And she felt him draw the sheet over her damp body.

She floated, rocked by some deep and tideless sea, her body still tingling from the force of its enrapturement.

She realised that Mick had returned to lie beside her. She reached out a drowsy hand and encountered bare skin.

Her eyes opened. 'Oh.'

'Oh?' There was a smile in his voice, but his face was serious and very intent. He took the welcoming hand and guided it down his body. 'Touch me,' he whispered. 'Hold me.'

At first her compliance was tentative, but she gradually became more confident, encouraged by his small groans of pleasure as she caressed him.

He kissed her hotly, his tongue gliding against hers. His fingers stroked her breasts, moulding them, coaxing them to renewed delight.

His hands strayed the length of her body, delineating the

long supple back, the slender curves of her hips, and thighs. Where they lingered.

Kate was trembling suddenly, aware that the same delicious excitement was overtaking her again. Beginning, incredibly, to build inside her.

She was lying facing him, and Mick's hands slid under her flanks, raising her slightly towards him. He kissed her mouth gently.

He said, 'Take me—please, my dove. My beautiful girl.'

She brought him into her slowly, the breath catching in her throat as she realised how simple it really was—how right. And just how much she had wanted to feel all that silken strength and potency inside her. To possess, and be possessed.

'Do I hurt you?' His whisper was urgent.

'No.' Her answer was a sigh. 'Ah, no.'

His movements were gentle at first, and smoothly, rhythmically controlled. And all the time he was watching her, she realised. Looking into her eyes. Observing the play of colour in her face. Listening for any change in her breathing.

And she smiled at him, her eyes luminous.

He hesitated, then moved away from her.

'What's the matter?' She stared at him in shocked bewilderment. 'Did—did I do something wrong?'

'No, *matia mou*.' He stroked her cheek reassuringly. 'I need to protect you, that is all.'

When he turned back, he lifted himself over her, entering her in one strong, fluid movement. She wound her arms round his neck, and, instinctively, lifted her legs to clasp him closer.

The rhythm he was imposing was more powerful now, and she joined it, moving with him in breathless unison.

She could feel the first, elusive blossoming of pleasure, and clung to him, striving for it. Demanding it.

The next moment, her whole being was convulsed in a fierce and scalding rapture. She cried out in ecstatic surprise, and heard Michael answer her as his own body shuddered into climax.

When she could speak, she said, 'Is it always like that?'

'Always with you, *agapi mou*.' He smoothed the hair back from her damp forehead, then wrapped her in his arms. She curled against him, sated and languid, and felt his cheek rest against her hair.

There was a silence, then he spoke, his voice barely a whisper. 'Marry me.'

She turned her head, and stared at him, her eyes wide, and her lips parted. 'You don't mean that.'

'I am perfectly serious,' he told her. 'I am asking you to be my wife, Katharina *mou*.'

'But you can't,' she said, almost wildly. 'It's ridiculous. I—I don't belong to your world.'

'We have just made our own world, *agapi mou*. I want no other.'

'But your family,' she protested. 'They'll expect you to marry some heiress.'

'My father lives his life.' His voice was oddly harsh. 'And I live mine. I wish to spend it with you.' He paused. 'But perhaps you don't want me?'

She said, 'I think I've wanted you since that first night on Zycos. And, yes, I'll marry you, Kyrios Michalis.'

He framed her face in his hands, and kissed her deeply, almost reverently.

He said, 'We should celebrate. I'll call room service and tell them to bring champagne.'

She smiled up at him. 'And strawberries?'

'You remember that, hmm?' He threw the covering sheet aside and got out of bed, stretching unselfconsciously.

Watching him, Kate felt her mouth go dry, and her throat tighten.

She said, 'Of course. But I couldn't understand why you didn't just—seduce me, there and then.'

Mick picked up a red silk robe from a chair and slipped it

on. He said softly, 'But I have been seducing you, *agapi mou*, every moment we have spent together since I first saw you. Don't you know that.'

He blew her a teasing kiss and walked away into the sitting room.

Two weeks later they were married in a quiet registry office ceremony with Sandy and Iorgos Vasso as witnesses.

They spent a brief honeymoon on Bali, then flew back to New York where Mick was supervising the completion of the latest Regina hotel.

'Does he usually take so personal an interest?' Kate asked Iorgos, who had soon become a friend.

'This is particularly important to him,' Iorgos admitted. 'There are elements on the board who have always been opposed to any expansion outside the Mediterranean, or indeed to any kind of change,' he added drily. 'It is no longer a foregone conclusion that he will succeed his father as chairman of the board when Ari eventually retires. So, Michalis needs a proven success to overcome the doubters.'

'I see.' Kate paused. 'Is his father one of the doubters?'

'That is something you should ask your husband, *kyria*.'

'I have.' Kate sighed. 'I asked him, too, when we'd be going to Greece so that I could meet his family, and he just changed the subject.'

She shook her head. 'He never talks about family things. Why, I didn't even know his mother had been a native New Yorker until I discovered we were living in her old home.'

'Does it make a difference?'

'No, but I'd like to have been told. And I wish he'd discuss this estrangement with his father, because I know it exists.'

He said gently, 'You are a very new wife, *kyria*. Maybe Mick feels you have enough adjustments to make for now. Enjoy the happiness you find in each other, and leave any problems for another day.'

And with that, she had to be content.

The apartment, in an exclusive district, was a sumptuous,

gracious place, all high ceilings, and rich wood panelling, and Kate had loved it on sight.

Mick gave her *carte blanche* to change anything she wanted but, in the end, she altered very little, replacing some carpets and curtains, and introducing a lighter colour scheme for their bedroom.

'I'm saving my energies for the nursery,' she told him happily.

'Well, there is no hurry for that.' He kissed her. 'Unless I am not enough for you,' he added softly.

The hotel was completed by Easter, and Kate, smiling confidently to conceal her inner trepidation, cut the ribbon which declared the New York Regina open for business.

It was barely a week later when she returned from a shopping trip to find a full-scale row in progress, with Mick pacing the drawing room, his face set and thunderous, while Iorgos tried unavailingly to calm him.

'What's happened?' Kate put down her packages, alarmed.

'We have been sent for,' Mick flung at her.

'Mr Theodakis has requested Michael to bring you to Kefalonia,' Iorgos explained more temperately.

'Is that such a bad thing?' Kate felt her way cautiously, keeping a wary eye on her husband's angry face. 'After all, we were bound to pay a visit eventually—weren't we?'

Mick snorted in exasperation, and stalked over to the window.

'It would not be wise to refuse,' Iorgos said quietly. 'Consider that, Michalis.'

'I have,' Mick said curtly, without looking round. 'And I know it must be done.'

For the first time in their marriage, he did not come to bed that night. Kate, disturbed, found him in the drawing room, slumped on a sofa with a decanter of whisky for company.

She had never seen him like this, she thought, as she knelt beside him. 'Darling, what's wrong? Talk to me, please.'

He looked at her, his eyes weary, and frighteningly distant.

'The reality I once spoke of, *pedhi mou*. It has found us. Now leave me. I need to be on my own—to think.'

And she had turned and gone back to their room, alone and suddenly scared.

CHAPTER SEVEN

KATE'S first glimpse of Kefalonia had been from the company private jet.

In spite of the uneasiness of the previous week, she couldn't repress a tingle of anticipation as she looked down on the rocky landscape beneath her.

Maybe, she thought, things will change now we're here. Go back to the way they were.

Because, ever since his father's summons, there'd been a strange new tension between Mick and herself which she seemed powerless to dispel, however much she tried.

Now, when he made love to her, he seemed remote, almost clinical in the ways in which he gave her pleasure. The warmth, the teasing, the laughter that had made their intimacy so precious was suddenly missing.

For the first time it was almost a relief that Mick still insisted on using protection during lovemaking, because she didn't want their baby to be conceived in an atmosphere like this.

She'd been surprised too when Mick told her to pack summer clothes and swimwear.

'But it's only April.' She stared at him. 'How long will we be staying on Kefalonia?'

'I am Greek, Katharina.' His voice was cold. 'The Villa Dionysius is my home.'

She said quietly, 'I'm sorry. I thought your home was with me. But I'll pack for an indefinite stay if that's what you want.'

His smile was brief and wintry. 'Thank you.'

She'd read as much as she could about the island and its history, prior to setting out, and knew that, because of the devastation caused by the earthquake which had struck in 1953, most of its buildings were comparatively modern.

But the Theodakis family home, the Villa Dionysius, had somehow survived. And soon she would be there.

Again she was aware of an odd prickle of nervousness, but told herself she was being ridiculous. Mick and his father might have been at odds in the past, but now a reconciliation was clearly indicated, and maybe her marriage was going to be the means of bringing that about. Which had to be a good thing—didn't it?

When they reached the villa, her spirits rose. It was a large rambling single-storied house, white-walled, with a faded terracotta roof. Flowering vines and climbing shrubs hung in festoons over the door and windows, and the garden was already bright with colour.

The whole place, she thought, had an air of timelessness about it, as if it had grown out of the headland on which it stood amid its encircling pine trees.

As she got out of the car, Kate could smell the resin, and hear the rasp of cicadas in the sunlit, windy air. Through the trees, she could see the turquoise sea far below, dancing with foam-capped waves.

She thought, 'I was crazy to worry. This is paradise.'

As she turned to look at the villa, the big door swung open, and a woman stood, dramatically framed in the doorway. She was tall and slim, with black hair that hung like a shining curtain down her back. Her skin was magnolia pale, and her almond-shaped eyes were tilted slightly at the corners. Her smiling mouth was painted a deep, sexy crimson, and in her figure-hugging white dress, she looked like some exotic, tropical flower.

Kate's throat tightened in instant, shocked recognition. She was aware of Mick standing rigidly beside her, his face like stone.

For a moment the newcomer stayed where she was, as if allowing them to fully appreciate the picture she made.

'Welcome home, *cher*.' Her voice was low-pitched and throaty. 'You shouldn't have stayed away so long.'

She walked to where Mick was standing, twining her arms round his neck, and kissing him on the lips.

'Mmm,' she murmured as she stood back. 'You taste so good—but then you always did.'

She looked at Kate. 'And this is your new wife.' Her eyes flickered over the suit in dark-green silk with a matching camisole that Kate had worn for the journey, and her smile widened. 'Won't you introduce me?'

'I already know who you are,' Kate said steadily. 'You're—Victorine.'

Not gone to ground, as Sandy had said, she thought, her heart pounding sickly, but here on Kefalonia, living in Mick's home…

But how? Why?

'I'm flattered.' Victorine laughed. 'On the other hand, you, *chère*, came as a complete surprise to—all of us.' She looked at Mick, pouting in reproof. 'Your father wasn't very pleased with you.'

Mick said harshly, 'When was he ever?' He paused. 'Where is he?'

Victorine shrugged. 'Waiting in the *saloni*. It's quite a family gathering. But you must promise me not to quarrel with him again. Though I'm sure you'll be on your best behaviour—now that you are married.'

Kate said, coolly and clearly, 'It was a long flight. I think I'd like to take a shower and change before any more introductions.'

'But of course.' Victorine turned to Mick. 'You have your usual suite in the West wing, *cher*.' She paused. 'Is there any particular room you would like Katherine to have?'

Mick said coldly, 'My wife sleeps with me.'

The slanting brows lifted. 'How sweet—and domestic.' She smiled at Katherine. 'You have managed to tame him, *chère*. I congratulate you.' She lowered her voice confidentially. 'Michael used to hate to share his bed for the whole night with anyone.'

Kate smiled back at her. 'Well,' she said lightly. 'That proves I'm not just—anyone.'

She walked sedately beside Mick through the wide passages, but under her calm exterior she was seething with a mixture of emotions. Anger was paramount, with bewilderment a close second.

At the end of one corridor were wide double doors, heavily carved. Mick opened them silently, and ushered her through. Kate found herself in an airy spacious sitting room, furnished in dramatic earth colours, with low sofas clustering round a table in heavy glass cut in the shape of a hexagon.

Beyond it was the bedroom, its vast bed draped in a coverlet the colour of green olives, which matched the long curtains at the windows.

Mick strode across the room, and opened another door. He said, 'The bathroom is here. You will find everything you need.'

'Including honesty?' Her voice shook. 'And some straight talking?'

Mick took off his jacket and tossed it across a chair.

He said shortly, 'Katharina—we are both jetlagged and out of temper, and I am shortly to have a difficult interview with my father. Oblige me by postponing this discussion.'

She said, 'No, I think I deserve an explanation now.' She began to wriggle out of her suit.

His mouth tightened. 'What do you wish to know?'

She stared at him. 'You and Victorine—you were lovers. You—you don't deny that.'

'No,' he said coldly. 'I do not. And isn't it a little late to start making my past an issue?'

'Yet now I find her—here—in your home.' She spread her hands. 'Why?'

'She is my father's mistress.' His tone was harsh. 'Does that satisfy your curiosity?'

Kate shook her head. 'You mean you passed her on—when you had finished with her?'

'No,' he said. 'I do not mean that. Victorine makes her own choices. And so does my father.'

'Did you—love her?'

His brows lifted mockingly. 'You have seen her, *agapi mou*,' he drawled. 'It must be clear what I felt for her.'

'And—now?'

'Now, I am with you, *pedhi mou*.'

She stared at him. Her voice was almost a whisper. 'Why did you marry me?'

He said, 'For a whole number of reasons.' He looked her over, standing in front of him, wearing only a few scraps of silk and lace, and his mouth twisted. 'And this is only one of them.'

Two strides brought him to her. Before she could resist, he picked her up in his arms and carried her to the bed.

She was beating at his chest with her fists. 'Put me down,' she ordered breathlessly. 'Do you hear.'

'Willingly.' Mick tossed her on to the mattress, following her down with total purpose, deftly unfastening his clothing.

'No.' Kate struggled, trying ineffectively to push him away. 'Don't you dare. I won't...'

'No, my Kate?' The dark eyes challenged her, laughter dancing outrageously in their depths. 'And how are you going to stop me?'

He bent to her, pushing the lacy cup away from her breast with his lips, and allowing his tongue to tease her uncovered nipple, while his hand slid under the silken rim of her briefs.

She said his name on a little sob, and her arms went round her neck, her body opening in heated, moist surrender as he entered her.

When the storm was over, Kate lay beneath him, drained and boneless.

'What happened?' Her voice was a shadow.

'My new cure for jet lag, *agapi mou*.' He kissed the tip of her nose. 'I may patent it.'

'You'll make another fortune,' she said weakly. 'I don't think I'll ever move again.'

'Unfortunately, you must. We have a shower to take, and my father to meet.' He sat up, raking the sweat-dampened hair back from his forehead. 'He will not appreciate waiting much longer,' he added with a touch of grimness.

'Yes,' she said. 'Of course.' She watched him disappear into the bathroom and gave a happy sigh, stretching languidly.

Then paused. Because, in reality, she thought frowning, she was no wiser about Victorine—or Mick's relationship with her, past or present.

Her concerns had been smothered by the most passionate lovemaking she'd experienced for days, but they hadn't been answered.

And I need answers, she thought, and shivered.

Aristotle Theodakis was standing by the window of the *saloni* as they came in, a dark figure against the sunlit vista of the sea outside. He turned to regard them frowningly, his whole stance radiating power and a certain aggression.

He was not as tall as his son, Kate saw, but more ruggedly built. His thick hair was silver, and his eyes were brilliant and piercing beneath their heavy brows.

He was undoubtedly a handsome, charismatic man, Kate thought, as she walked across the room towards him, her hand clasped firmly in Mick's. But she was still amazed that Victorine could have abandoned the son for the father.

She glanced around her, trying to assimilate something of her surroundings. The *saloni* was a vast room, but furnished with comfort rather than overt luxury. The colours were cool, and clear, and the walls and surfaces uncluttered. One of the few embellishments was a large portrait of a dark-haired woman with a serene face positioned above the huge, empty fireplace, which Kate assumed was the late Regina Theodakis.

She was aware of other people in the room too—a tall fair-haired woman standing quietly beside the fireplace, and, at her side, a much younger girl, with dark hair and eyes, her vibrantly pretty face spoiled by a sullen expression.

Mick halted a couple of yards from his father and inclined his head, coolly and unsmilingly. 'Papa.'

Aristotle Theodakis did not even glance at Kate. He said in his own language, 'I have spent months trying to prevent my daughter from making a fool of herself over some penniless nobody. Now, my son does the same thing. I had other plans for you, Michalis.'

Before Mick could reply, Kate said in her clear, careful Greek, 'Perhaps your children are old enough to decide their own fates, *kyrie*.'

His head turned abruptly towards her, and she waited to be blasted out of existence. Instead, he said slowly, '*Po, po po*. So, you speak our tongue?'

'Not very well. But Michael has been teaching me.'

'Hmm.' He looked her over, slowly, as if something puzzled him, taking in the simple cream dress she'd changed into. 'Perhaps he is not as stupid as I thought.'

He stepped forward, opening his arms imperatively and, after a brief hesitation, Mick returned his embrace.

'Sit down.' He waved Kate towards one of the wide, deeply cushioned sofas which flanked a low table. 'Ismene will pour you some iced tea. And for the sake of your wife and Linda, we will speak English, Michalis.'

He indicated the fair woman. 'Katharina—this is my late wife's cousin, Linda Howell. She used to be my daughter's companion.'

'And she still could be,' Ismene said petulantly, pouring the tea into tall glasses. 'Why can't I go and live in her house at Sami?'

'Because she would be too soft with you,' her father

growled. 'You would be running off to meet Petros Alessou all the time, and she would do nothing to stop you.'

'It's hard to object to Ismene meeting with a young man she's known since childhood.' Linda's voice was quiet, with a slight American drawl. She gave Kate a rueful look as she came to sit beside her. 'I'm afraid you've walked into an ongoing problem.'

'There is no problem,' Ari Theodakis scowled. 'Ismene does not see the Alessou boy, and that is final.' He snorted. 'A newly qualified doctor, with only his ideals in the bank. A fine match for my daughter. And the problems it has caused with his father.' He threw up his hands. 'I haven't had a decent game of backgammon in weeks.'

He looked at Kate. 'Do you play?'

'No,' lied Kate who had seen the speed and ferocity that the Greeks brought to the game, and didn't fancy her chances.

'Then Michalis can teach you that too—in the evenings while you are waiting for my grandson to be born.'

There was a sudden devastating silence. Kate gasped. 'Mr Theodakis—there isn't—I'm not...' She paused, aware her cheeks were burning, and turned to Mick whose expression was like stone.

'Of course not,' Linda said soothingly. 'Ari—you're impossible,' she added sternly. 'Why, the children are still on honeymoon.'

His shrug was unrepentant. 'Then why the hasty marriage?'

'Because there was no reason to wait.' Mick's tone was silky, but there was danger in it too. 'And I thought, Papa, that you wished me to be married—settled in life. You—and your supporters on the Theodakis board.'

'I did. I do.' Ari Theodakis frowned. 'But a man needs children to give him real stability.'

'Yes,' Mick said quietly. 'But in our own good time—not yours.'

'Well, it's just not fair,' Ismene burst out. 'I'm not allowed to see Petros, yet Michalis has married someone without money, and Papa did not interfere.'

Mick's face relaxed slightly. 'Only because I did not give him the opportunity, little sister.'

'So you can marry a penniless nobody, and I am expected to take Spiros Georgiou just because his family is rich. A man who wears glasses and has damp hands, besides being shorter than I am.'

There was real unhappiness mingled with the outrage in Ismene's voice and Kate bit back her involuntary smile.

'And you will mind your tongue, my girl,' her father cautioned sternly. 'Or go to your room.'

Ismene set down the jug with a crash. 'It will be a pleasure,' she retorted, and flounced from the room.

Kate heard Linda Howell sigh softly.

She said, 'Katherine, shall we take our tea out on the terrace and leave the men to talk?'

Kate forced a smile. 'That would be good.'

The terrace was wide and bordered by an elaborate balustrade. Kate leaned on the sun-warmed stone and took a deep breath, as she looked down through the clustering pines to the ripple of the sea. 'It's beautiful.'

Linda smiled. 'It's also a minefield,' she said wryly. 'As you must have noticed.'

'Yes.' Kate bit her lip. 'Has there—always been friction between Mick and his father.'

'Not when Regina was alive, although I know she could foresee problems when Mick became fully adult and challenged Ari's authority.

'Is that her portrait over the fireplace?'

'Yes.' Linda's mouth tightened. 'I'm surprised it's still there. Each time I visit, which isn't often these days, I expect to find it's been consigned to some cellar.'

'You and Regina were close?'

'We were raised together. My father was a career diplomat,

and always on the move, so I stayed in New York with my aunt and uncle. Regina and I were more like sisters than cousins. When she married Ari, the villa became a second home for me. After she died so suddenly, it seemed natural to stay on and care for Ismene.' Her blue eyes were sad. 'And apart from that Ari and I could help each other grieve.'

'How did she die?'

'She had this heart weakness. It was incredible because she was the strongest person I knew—she was a marvellous rider, and she sailed and played tennis like a champion. But she had a really hard time when Michael was born, and the doctors warned her against any more pregnancies. But she and Ari had always wanted a daughter, so she decided to take the risk.' She shook her head. 'She was never really well afterwards and one day—she just went.'

She pursed her lips ruefully. 'I wish, for her sake, I'd done a better job with Ismene, but each time I tried to impose rules, Ari would undermine them. He wanted Ismene to be a free spirit like her mother. What he didn't grasp was that Regina's freedom came from self-discipline. Now he's trying to close the dam, and it could be too late.'

'Because of this Petros?' Kate drank some of her tea. 'You think they should be allowed to marry?'

'He's a great guy, and she's known him for ever. I always guessed that one day she'd stop looking on him as just another big brother, and she could have made so many worse choices.' She sighed. 'But she approached it the wrong way. She should have let Ari think it was all his idea. Just before you arrived, she demanded that Petros come to tonight's family dinner as her future husband.' Linda pulled a wry face. 'I tried to talk her out of it. The Theodakis men do not respond well to ultimatums.'

'I'd noticed.' Kate set her glass down on the balustrade. 'Mick's been in an odd mood ever since his father sent for us.' She paused. 'Of course there could be another reason for that,' she added carefully.

'Ah,' Linda said. 'So you've met Ari's other house guest?'

'Yes.' Kate stared hard at the view.

Linda sighed. 'If you want me to give an explanation, I can't. She was with Mick, now she's with Ari. End of story.'

Kate caught a sudden glimpse of pain on the calm face, and realised she'd stumbled on a different story altogether.

'But whatever happened,' Linda went on after a pause. 'Mick married you, and not the dynastic heiress his father would have chosen.' She gave Kate a swift smile. 'Maybe we'd better check on them—see there's no blood on the floor.'

'Is there really that much friction?' Kate asked, troubled.

'It's natural.' Linda shrugged. 'Mick's the heir apparent, and he has a lot of support in the company, but Ari's still king, and he's not ready to abdicate—not by a mile. They'll work it out.' She paused. 'And if things get too heavy, you can always retreat to the beach house.'

She pointed downwards through the trees to a splash of terracotta. 'Ari had it built for when there was an extra influx of guests, but Regina really made it her own place. He was away a lot, and she found the villa big and lonely without him. It has its own pool, and this wonderful platform overlooking the sea where she used to sit and paint.'

She glanced at her watch, and uttered a faint exclamation. 'Hey, I must be off.'

'Aren't you staying for dinner?' Dismayed, Kate took the hand she was offered.

'No, I was asked to meet you, which I've done, and now I'm going home.' She smiled at Kate. 'I hope you'll come and visit at Sami. Get Ismene to bring you over. You didn't see her best side today, but she has a lot going for her. And she could do with a friend.'

'Perhaps,' Kate thought as she watched her go. 'Ismene isn't the only one.'

She turned back to look down at the beach house. It sounded as if it could become a sanctuary. Tomorrow, she

decided, she would find her way down there. Ask Ismene to show her the way perhaps.

She heard the sound of voices, and Mick and his father emerged from the *saloni* and came to join her.

'Has Linda gone?' Mick put his arm round her, resting his hand casually on her hip.

'Yes, you've just missed her.'

'I asked her to stay for dinner.' There was a touch of defensiveness in Ari's tone. 'But she said she had plans.'

'Well, perhaps she did.' Mick shrugged. 'I hope so. She's a very beautiful woman.'

There was a silence, then Ari turned to Kate. 'Well, *pedhi mou*. Do you think you will be happy here?'

'I'm happy to be wherever Michael is,' she returned quietly.

'Good—good.' He smiled. 'I am glad my son is proving an attentive husband.'

The colour deepened in Kate's cheeks, but she returned his gaze without wavering. 'I have no major complaints, *kyrie*.'

Mick looked at her, his mouth relaxing into a faint smile. He said softly, 'You will suffer for that tonight, my girl.'

'Well restrain your ardour until after dinner,' Ari said with sudden joviality. 'Androula is preparing her special lemon chicken and she will not forgive if you are late.'

He clapped Mick on the shoulder. 'It will be like old times, *ne*?'

Mick looked at the sea, his face expressionless. 'As you say.'

They're like a pair of dogs, Kate thought uneasily, circling each other, getting in the odd nip. But the main event is still to come.

'I thought tomorrow I would ask your sister to show me around,' she said later, when she was alone with Mick in their bedroom, changing for dinner. 'Get to know her.'

'A word of advice,' Mick said, adjusting his black tie.

'Don't get drawn into Ismene's intrigues. They always end in tears.'

'I'm not,' Kate protested. She was sitting at the dressing table in bra and briefs putting the finishing touches to her makeup. 'But your father's choice of a husband for her doesn't sound very appealing.'

'Don't worry about it. There will be no enforced marriage.' He paused. 'Your hair looks beautiful.'

'Someone called Soula did it.' Kate touched the artfully careless topknot with a self-conscious hand. 'Apparently your father sent her to look after me. She did all our unpacking, too, and would have helped me dress if I'd let her.'

'Then I'm glad you sent her away,' Mick said softly. 'I wish to retain some privileges.' He went into the adjoining dressing room, and emerged a moment later with a length of black silk draped over his arm. 'Wear this tonight, *agapi mou*.'

'Really?' Kate's brows lifted doubtfully. It was an elegant bias-cut dress with a low neck and shoestring straps that he'd bought her in New York. 'Isn't that a little much for a family dinner. I—I can't wear a bra with it.'

'I know.' He undid the tiny clip, and slipped off the scrap of lace. 'So—have this in its place.'

It was a diamond, cut in a classic tear-drop shape, and glowing like captured fire against her skin. Kate gasped in disbelief, as Mick fastened the fine gold chain round her neck. Her voice shook. 'It's—beautiful.'

His eyes met hers in the mirror. 'But the setting,' he told her gently, 'is even more exquisite.' And for a tingling moment, his hands grazed the tips of her bare breasts. 'A jewel,' he whispered. 'For my jewel.'

He dropped a kiss on her shoulder and straightened. 'Stand up, *matia mou*.'

She obeyed, and he dropped the black dress deftly over her head, without disturbing a strand of hair, and zipped it up.

She said unsteadily, 'You are—almost too good at that.'

Laughing, he took her hand. 'You inspire me, my Kate.'

Then why don't you tell me you love me? she wondered fiercely. Because you never have. Not once in all these months.

When she entered the *saloni* on Mick's arm, she found it deserted apart from Ismene who was glancing through a fashion magazine beside the log fire which had been kindled to fight the evening chill. The younger girl looked up. 'Michalis, Papa wishes you to go to him in his study. There has been a fax you should see.'

'Very well,' Mick said. 'But look after Katharina for me. Get her a drink—and call her no names,' he added grimly.

Ismene came over to her with an ouzo, looking subdued.

'I wish to apologise, sister. I was rude when I called you a penniless nobody. Although Papa said it first,' she added, her brow darkening.

Kate laughed. 'Let's forget it and begin again, shall we?'

'I would like that. But I cannot help being jealous, because Michalis has married whom he wishes, and I may not.' She gave Kate a speculative look. 'You are not like his other women,' she offered.

Kate's smile held constraint. 'I've noticed.'

Ismene giggled. 'So you have met her. I wish I had been there. How she must hate you.'

Kate said slowly, 'But—that's all in the past now—surely?'

'Is it?' The pretty face was suddenly cynical. 'Maybe. Who knows?'

Kate struggled with herself and lost. 'How did Victorine come to be with your father?'

Ismene shrugged. 'It is a mystery. We thought at first that she had come to wait for Michalis—to be with him when he returned. We could not believe that Papa had invited her—and that she was his *eromeni* instead.'

She shook her head. 'And when Michalis did come, he was so angry—like a crazy man. We could hear him with Papa, shouting at each other.' She shuddered. 'Terrible things were said.'

'Did he care about her so much?' Kate concentrated fiercely on her drink.

Ismene shrugged. 'Naturally. She was the ultimate trophy woman, and Papa took her from him.

She brightened. 'But now you and Mick are married, he need not stay away any more. Because he cannot still be in love with Victorine, and Papa need not be jealous.'

'No.' Kate said quietly, her throat tightening. 'It's all—worked out very well.'

'I wish life could be as good for me. Do you know that Papa will not even allow my Petros to come to the house any more.' She tossed her head. 'But it makes no difference, because we are still engaged to each other.'

Kate picked her words carefully. 'Perhaps your father feels you're still young to be making such an important decision.'

Ismene snorted disrespectfully. 'I am the same age as Mama when Papa married her. And I would not be too young if I agreed to marry that horrid Spiro. Although I would rather die.'

Kate's face relaxed into a grin. 'I'd say you had a point,' she conceded.

Ismene looked at her hopefully. 'Perhaps Mick would speak to Papa for me. Talk him round?'

Kate gave a constrained smile, but did not answer because at that moment Victorine entered the *saloni*. She was wearing another clinging dress in fuchsia pink, its low-cut bodice glittering with crystals.

She helped herself to a drink, then came across to Kate, her eyes fixed on the diamond pendant.

'A new necklace, *chère*?' She ignored Ismene. Her mouth smiled, but her eyes were venomous. 'Men usually buy their

wives expensive gifts because they feel guilty about something. I wonder what Mick has on his conscience?'

'Bitch,' Ismene whispered succinctly as Victorine moved off towards the fire, using the distinctive swaying walk which had graced so many catwalks. 'Don't let her wind you up.'

Easier said than done, Kate thought wryly.

Ari gave her the place of honour beside him at dinner, and talked to her kindly, but she had the feeling she was being screened, so it wasn't the most comfortable meal she'd ever had.

It was undoubtedly one of the most delicious though, and she said so as she finished the famous chicken, fragrant with lemon.

'I'm glad you liked it.' He gave her an approving smile. 'From tomorrow, it will be for you to order the meals, *pedhi mou*, and run the household. I have instructed Androula, and Yannis my majordomo, to come to you for your orders each day.'

Kate stared at him. 'But I've never...'

'Then you must begin.' His tone demolished further protest, and alerted the attention of everyone round the table to Kate's embarrassment. 'You are the wife of my son, and you take your rightful place in his home.'

He gave Mick a fierce look, and received an unsmiling nod in reply.

'And don't keep me waiting too long for my grandson,' he added, more jovially, turning back to Kate, who looked down at her plate, blushing furiously, aware that Victorine was watching her.

It was a long meal and, afterwards, there was coffee in the *saloni*, and another hissed diatribe from Ismene about her father's injustice, and the general misery of her life.

In fact, meeting Linda had probably been the highlight of a rather fraught day, Kate thought, as she prepared for bed that night.

When she emerged from the bathroom, Mick was standing

by the window in his dressing gown, staring into the darkness.

She slid her arms round his waist. 'Coming to bed?'

'Presently.'

She rested her cheek against his chest. She said softly, a smile in her voice, 'Well, we have our instructions. Your father wants a grandchild.'

He detached himself from her embrace. He said coldly, 'Understand this, Katharina. I give orders. I do not take them. And now I intend to sleep.'

He took off his robe and tossed it over a chair, then walked, naked, to the bed, and got in, turning on his side so that his back was towards her for the first time in the marriage.

Leaving her standing there, shocked, bewildered and suddenly totally isolated. With Mick's diamond burning like ice between her breasts.

CHAPTER EIGHT

I BELIEVED, Kate thought flatly, that it wasn't possible to be more unhappy—more alone than I was that night. But what did I know?

She looked round the impersonal luxury of the hotel room she now occupied alone, and shivered.

She should have realised, she thought. Made the connection there and then. Seen that her brief marriage had begun to collapse—and faced the reason.

Yet, on that following morning, when she'd woken to find herself in his arms, and heard him whisper, 'I'm sorry, *agapi mou*. Forgive me...' she'd been able to tell herself it was just a temporary glitch. That he'd had a difficult day too.

And she'd drawn him down to her, her lips parting willingly under his kiss.

Of course, Kate thought flatly, as the memories stung at her mind, I didn't realise just how much there was to forgive.

Because I was never a real wife—just a red herring, intended to draw his father away from the truth about his relationship with Victorine. The solution to a problem, just as I heard him discussing with Iorgos that night on Zycos.

And Mick didn't want us to have a child because he knew the marriage wasn't going to last. At least he didn't pretend about that.

And that, too, is why he never said he loved me. It was as near as he could get to honesty.

She heard herself moan, softly and painfully. She got up from the bed and began to pace restlessly round the room, then paused, and took a deep breath.

She shouldn't be doing this to herself, and she knew it. It was all still too new. Too raw.

After all, less than two months ago, she'd still been living in her fool's paradise.

And soon now she would be back on Kefalonia, and all the old wounds would be open and bleeding again.

She would have to stand in the village church, and watch Ismene make her marriage vows to the man she loved, and see Petros' rather serious face alight with tenderness as he looked at her.

And she would have to see Mick and Victorine together, exchanging their secret lovers' glances. Become part of the betrayal she had run from. Until Mick chose to let her go.

I can't do it, she thought, nausea acrid in her throat. No one should be expected to play a part like that. Pretend...

But no matter how battered she felt—how emotionally bruised—she couldn't deny the magic of those first weeks she'd spent on Kefalonia.

Beginning at breakfast that first morning when Ismene, eyes dancing, told her that Victorine was no longer at the villa.

'She's on her way to Paris to do some shopping,' she confided. 'To buy a bigger diamond than yours, Katharina *mou*,' she added naughtily.

Kate tried to look reproving. 'Has your father gone with her?'

'No, no.' Ismene looked shocked. 'Because there will be meetings soon with some of the other directors of our companies. Last time Victorine was *so* bored.' She rolled her eyes. 'She likes the money, you understand, but she is not interested in how it is made. Maybe this is why Papa encouraged her to go,' she went on. 'Or perhaps he is still not quite sure...' She stopped, guiltily, her eyes flying to Kate's suddenly frozen face. 'But no—that is silly.'

'Yes,' Kate agreed quietly. 'Very silly.'

'And, of course, you will be Papa's hostess—to prove to everyone that he and Mick are friends again.' Ismene went on eagerly. 'There has been much anxiety, you understand,

and people have taken sides, which is not good. But everything will be better now.'

'I hope so.' Kate forced a smile. 'Perhaps Victorine won't come back.'

'But she will.' Ismene pulled a face. 'Unless she finds a richer man than Papa.'

Whatever the reasons for it, Kate couldn't be sorry about Victorine's absence, especially when days lengthened into weeks with no sign of her return.

Not that she had time to brood about anything. Her new responsibilities had not been exaggerated, she discovered from the moment Yannis and Androula took her on the promised tour of the house.

The Villa Dionysius was much larger than even her first impression had suggested—a positive labyrinth of passages, courtyards and rooms, and Kate saw all of it, down to the cellars, the food stores and the linen cupboards.

'Each generation has added to the house,' Yannis told her proudly. 'And you and Kyrios Michalis will do the same—when the children come.'

Kate bit back a smile. It was ridiculous, she thought, the way everyone was trying to prompt them into parenthood. And what a pity she couldn't share the joke with Mick.

She couldn't help being nervous as the first of the promised guests began to arrive, but was able to draw on her training as a courier to give each of them a composed and smiling welcome, and make sure their comfort was catered for in every way.

It was not an easy time. Not all the meetings went smoothly, and she was aware of tensions and undercurrents as people came and went. Both Mick and his father were grim and thoughtful at times.

But at last, all the visitors departed, and Kate, their compliments still ringing in her ears, was able to draw breath.

'You have done well, *pedhi mou*,' Ari told her. He gave a satisfied smile. 'In fact, it has all been most successful.' He

darted a glance at Mick. 'And I am not quite ready for Yeronitsia, *ne*?'

'Yeronitsia?' Kate repeated puzzled.

'A high rock near Ayios Thomas,' Mick supplied unsmilingly. 'From which, legend says, the old and useless used to be thrown. My father,' he added, 'likes to joke.'

But Kate couldn't feel it had been a joke. And a few days later, when Linda took her on a tour of the island, she mentioned it, while they were sitting drinking coffee on the waterfront at Fiscardo.

Linda sighed. 'You're right, it's not funny, but I guess it was inevitable. Ari was so pleased and proud when Mick joined the company, but less so as he began to find his own voice—formulate his own ideas.'

She shrugged. 'You can understand it. Ari was proud of what he'd achieved, and was wary of change—especially the kind of expansion Mick was advocating. Also,' her smile was wry, 'he was beginning to feel his age, and he resented this. He began to say that Mick was too young—too wild to step into his shoes. That the Theodakis corporation should not go to someone with such a high-profile social life. And for a time there, Mick supplied him with all the ammunition he needed,' she added ruefully.

'And, Ari likes to play games—to hint at his retirement in private, then deny it in public. But there've been signs that the board is getting restive—that support for Michael is growing. I—I hope Ari goes with dignity before he's forced out. It would have broken Regina's heart to know how far things had deteriorated between them,' she added huskily.

She didn't speak Victorine's name, but then she didn't have to, Kate thought with a sudden chill.

And one day soon the beautiful Creole would return.

But, in the meantime, Kate could relax and enjoy herself. Already the Villa Dionysius was beginning to feel like home. The staff were so well-trained that the house almost ran itself, and this gave her the opportunity to explore the rest of the

island, sometimes with Linda, but usually and joyfully in Mick's company, making the most of its many beauties before the influx of tourists arrived.

She loved hearing him talk about Kefalonia's sometimes stormy history, and share his knowledge of the archaeological discoveries that had taken place over the years.

She was thrilled by the various underground caves with their dark and secret lakes that he showed her, but shivered away from the village of Markopoulo after Mick told her that the Church of Our Lady there was visited each August by crowds of small snakes.

'They crawl up to her icon,' Mick said, amused at her horrified expression. 'We look on them as good luck, especially as they stayed away during the last war, and in the earthquake year.'

'I prefer miracles that don't wriggle,' Kate said with dignity. 'I think I shall arrange to be somewhere else in August.'

Remembering those lightly spoken words now, Kate bit her lip until she tasted blood. Perhaps she shouldn't have been so flippant about the island's luck. Because hers had begun to run out not long afterwards.

Ismene's feud with her father over her wish to marry Petros had shown no signs of abating. Although she had been forbidden to see him, she continued to meet him in secret and, on several occasions, Kate had been her unwilling accomplice, driving her into Argostoli, the island's capital, on vague shopping expeditions.

Ismene had insisted on introducing them, and Kate had to admit that, apart from his lack of worldly goods, she couldn't fault him. He was more serious in his manner than Ismene, but blessed with a quiet sense of humour. He was also good looking, and intelligent.

'Papa says he is not good for me,' Ismene said soberly as they drove home. 'But, in truth, Katharina, he is much too good, and I know it. All the same, I will be a good and loving wife to him.'

Kate found herself unexpectedly touched to the heart by this little speech. But when she mentioned it to Mick, he was angry.

'I told you not to get involved,' he reminded her coldly. 'Now you are joining her in her deceit.'

They almost had a row about it, and matters did not improve when Ismene mounted another tearful and highly vocal campaign to get her father to approve her engagement.

Kate had not been altogether sorry when Mick had insisted on the move down to the peace of the beach house. It had already become one of her favourite places, and she had taken to swimming in the pool there every day anyway, now that the real summer heat had begun, but the sea was still cold.

It was much smaller than the villa, with just two bedrooms, a large living room, as well as a kitchen and bathroom, but it was furnished with exquisite comfort, and it had the great advantage of seclusion. And the big platform at the front that Linda had mentioned was perfect for sunbathing.

'A second honeymoon,' Kate said dreamily on their first evening alone there.

Mick raised his eyebrows. 'And less chance for you to become embroiled in Ismene's mischief, *matia mou*,' he told her, pulling her into his arms.

She was disappointed when she discovered that he was about to depart on visits to the Regina hotels on Corfu, Crete and Rhodes, and that she would not be going with him.

'It's pure routine. You'd be bored.' He'd kissed her swiftly as he left for the airport. 'Try not to let Ismene and Papa kill each other, and I'll be back before you know it.'

But she felt restless, edgy without him. The days were long, but the nights were longer, and his daily phone calls were only part consolation.

She had to put up with sulks from Ismene too, when the younger girl discovered that Kate was not going to drive her to any more secret rendezvous.

She began to spend more time at the beach house. Quite often she was joined there by Linda, and Ismene too when she regained her good humour, and Kate enjoyed preparing poolside lunches for them.

Regina Theodakis had clearly been keen on reading as well as painting, and a large, crammed bookcase was one of the features of the living room. Kate found herself making new discoveries every day, as well as renewing her acquaintance with some old favourites.

Mick had been gone almost two weeks, when Victorine returned. As soon as Kate walked into the villa she was aware of a subtle shift in the atmosphere. She didn't really need Ismene's whispered, 'She's back,' to know what had happened.

'And she's in a really good mood—all smiles,' Ismene went on disparagingly. 'You should see the luggage she's brought back. She must have bought the world. And she's given me a present.'

She extracted a silky top with shoestring straps and exquisite beading from a bag emblazoned with the name of a boutique from the exclusive Kolonaki Square in Athens, and held it up. 'See?'

Kate's brows rose. 'Very nice,' she commented drily. 'Perhaps she's going on a charm offensive.'

But her optimism was short-lived.

'The sun has given you some colour, *chère*.' Victorine was stretched out on a lounger on the terrace, wearing a miniscule string bikini, the expression in her eyes concealed behind designer sunglasses. 'That shade of hair can make a woman look so washed out,' she added disparagingly.

'And good morning to you, too,' Kate said coolly, pouring herself some fruit juice.

'So you are not pregnant yet.' Victorine began to apply a fresh layer of sun lotion to her arms. 'Ari is very disappointed. It might be wise not to keep him waiting too long, or he might begin to wonder about this marriage of yours.

Especially as Michalis has apparently become—restless again, and left you all alone here.'

'Mick's on a business trip,' Kate said, resisting the urge to throw the fruit juice over her antagonist. 'We don't have to be joined at the hip every moment of the day.'

'Or the night either.' Smilingly, Victorine recapped the bottle. 'You are very understanding to allow him these little diversions, *chère*. I hope your trust is rewarded. Michalis can be so wicked when he gets bored.'

'Well, you should know,' Kate said blandly, returning her glass to the tray, and walking off.

But even the pleasure of having the last word couldn't sweeten the little exchange for her.

'I'll keep out of the way,' she thought, thanking her stars that she had a sanctuary, but, to her dismay, Ari made it clear that he expected her to be present at dinner that evening, and perform her usual duties, so she reluctantly obeyed.

Victorine was in her element at dinner, her behaviour to Ari seductively possessive, as she regaled them with the latest film-world gossip, hinting at the lucrative contracts that were still being offered her.

'But how could I be away for months at a time, *cher*, when even a few weeks is too much.' Lips pouting, she put a caressing hand on Ari's arm.

Kate was just wondering what excuse she could make to avoid coffee in the *saloni* when the door of the dining room opened, and Mick walked in.

Amid the exclamations of astonishment and welcome, Kate got shakily to her feet.

'Why didn't you tell me?' she whispered, as he reached her.

'I wanted to surprise you, *agapi mou*.' His arms went round her, drawing her to him. His mouth was warm on hers. 'Have I succeeded?'

'Shall I tell Androula to bring you some food, boy?' Ari barked.

'I had an early dinner in Athens with Iorgos. Now I just want to wash off the city grime, and relax a little.' He smiled at Kate. 'Come and run a bath for me, *matia mou*,' he invited softly.

As Kate went with him, blushing, to the door, she was suddenly aware of Victorine watching her, her eyes cold with derision, and something oddly like pity…

'Was it a successful trip?' Kate lay in the circle of Mick's arms, as the scented water lapped round them.

'The homecoming is better.' He wound a long strand of her damp hair round his fingers and kissed it. 'Maybe, I should go away more often.'

'I disagree.' She touched his face gently with her hand, then paused. 'I didn't know you were going to Athens.'

'Nor did I, but it was unavoidable. A last-minute thing.' He picked up the sponge and squeezed warm water over her shoulders. 'So, what has been happening here? Has Ismene been behaving herself?'

'I try not to ask.' She bit her lip. 'Victorine came back this morning.'

'Leaving a trail of devastation in every design salon in Europe, no doubt.'

Had she imagined the fractional hesitation before his dismissive reply.

'She was shopping in Athens too,' she ventured.

'It's a big city, *agapi mou*.' He kissed the side of her neck. 'Now, let's dry ourselves. Our bed is waiting, and you can show me all over again how glad you are to see me.'

And Kate forgot everything—even that strange, niggling doubt—in the passionate bliss of their reunion.

But, with hindsight, she could have no doubt that Mick had been with Victorine in Athens. He'd brushed aside her tentative query, but he hadn't denied it.

And, however much she'd longed for his return, she

couldn't pretend it was all honey and roses in the days that followed.

Within twenty-four hours, it was evident that relations between Ari and himself were strained, and Mick seemed to retire into a tight-lipped, preoccupied world of his own.

More visiting executives came and went, and there was another endless stream of meetings. Kate struggled to fulfil her role as hostess, but found her smile beginning to crack after a while. She felt as if she was living on the edge of a volcano, but, when she tried to question Mick about what was going on, she found herself blocked.

'But I want to help,' she protested.

'You are helping.' He kissed the top of her head. 'Be content.'

But that was easier said than done.

Even when they made love, Kate had the feeling that he'd retreated emotionally behind some barrier, and she had to search for him, reach out to him, in the joining of their bodies.

But at least in the early afternoons she had him all to herself. They had gone down to the cove to swim at first, but then had found Victorine there, sunbathing in nothing but a thong. Mick ignored her stonily, but, when he found Ismene emulating her, he gave his sister a telling-off in cold, fierce Greek which reduced her to tears.

After that, they had stayed up at the beach house, and Mick had given strict orders that their privacy there was not to be disturbed by anyone. Even Ismene did not dare to intrude on them.

One hot and windless day, lying in the shelter of a poolside umbrella, Kate put down her book, and said, 'When are we going to have a baby?'

He was glancing frowningly through some papers. 'Has my father been asking again?'

'No,' she said. 'This time it's all my own idea. Michael— can we at least talk about it—please?'

His mouth tightened. 'This is not a good time for me, *pedhi mou*.' His voice was gentle but inflexible.

She swallowed. 'Then when can we have a discussion about our marriage—our future?'

He was silent for a moment. 'When I get back from America. We'll talk then.'

She sat up, staring at him. 'You're going to New York? When?'

'Next week. I shall be gone about ten days—perhaps less.'

She said breathlessly, 'Take me with you.'

'It's a business trip, Katharina,' he said. 'I shall be in meetings twelve hours a day. We would never see each other.'

'Mick—please. This is important to me.'

'And you are important here,' he said drily. 'I gather the household can't function without you.'

'That's nonsense, and you know it.' Her voice rose. 'The house runs like clockwork.'

'But you, *agapi mou*, wind the clock. My father is pleased with you.'

She said huskily, 'Is that why you're abandoning me here—to keep him sweet? He already has someone to fill that role.'

His tone was curt. 'Be careful what you say.'

'Michael.' Her voice appealed. 'I'm your wife. I want to be with you. Can't you understand that?'

'But you would not be with me,' he said. 'Because I should always be with other people.' He picked up his papers again. 'And I will soon be back.'

She said raggedly, 'This is why your mother used to stay here, isn't it? Not because it had wonderful views she could paint, but because the villa was too big and too lonely, and your father was always away on business as well. Maybe she even persuaded herself she didn't mind. But I do mind, Michael. I mind like hell.'

'Is it really such a penance to stay here?' He got to his

feet angrily. 'You live in comfort. The servants adore you. Ismene loves you as a sister in blood.'

'And your ex-mistress thinks I'm a bad joke.'

'Ah, Victorine,' he said softly. 'Somehow I knew the conversation would come round to her.'

'You can't pretend it's a normal situation.'

'But one we have to accept—for now, at least.' There was finality in his tone.

'Can you accept it?' She was frightened now, but she pushed herself on. Letting her darkest thoughts out into the harsh sunlight. 'Is that why we live down here, Michael—because you can't bear to see her—to think of her with your father? Tell me—tell me the truth.'

In spite of the intense heat, his glance chilled her. Silenced her. Made her heart flutter in panic.

'You are being absurd, Katharina. Unless you wish to make me angry, do not speak of this again.' He picked up his watch, and fastened it on to his wrist. 'I am going to shower, and drive into Argostoli. At the risk of being accused of abandonment,' he added cuttingly, 'I am not going to invite you to come with me.'

When he'd gone, she retrieved her book, and tried to read, but the words blurred and danced in front of her eyes. Her throat tightened painfully, and she thought, 'Oh, God, what have I said? What have I done.'

He returned while she was dressing for dinner—several scared, aching hours later. She'd put on the black dress he liked, and hung his diamond at her throat.

'Mick.' Her voice shook. 'I'm sorry. I didn't know what I was saying.'

He put his hands on her shoulders. In the mirror, she met his gaze, hooded, enigmatic.

He said, 'Perhaps we both have some thinking to do, Katharina. And my trip will give us the necessary space, *ne*?'

No, she thought. We don't need that. There's too much space between us already. I can't reach you any more.

But she smiled steadily, and said, 'I expect you're right.' And knew she was weeping inside.

Kate put her hands up to her face, wiping away the tears she did not have to hide any more.

Why did she have this total recall, she asked herself desperately, when amnesia would have been so much more merciful?

She thought I can't go on—torturing myself like this. I can't...

She went into the bathroom and washed her face, trying to conceal the signs of distress.

Then she went out into the sitting room. She would have to confront Michael once and for all. Tell him she'd changed her mind. That even if their divorce took for ever, she would not go back to Kefalonia and be made to relive any more of her humiliation and betrayal.

She was halfway across the room when his bedroom door opened and he came out. He was wearing dark, close-fitting pants, and a white shirt, with a silk tie knotted loosely round his throat. He was carrying a light cashmere jacket in a fine check over one arm, and fastening his cuff-links with his free hand as he walked.

He halted, his brows lifting. 'You should have stayed in your sanctuary a little longer, *matia mou*.' His tone was sardonic. 'Then you would have been spared the sight of me.'

'You're going out?'

'Evidently.'

'Where are you going?'

'Be careful. Katharina *mou*,' he said softly. 'You are beginning to sound like a wife. Although I am sure you do not wish to be treated as one.'

She flushed, biting her lip. 'It's just that—I need to talk to you.'

'But I am not in the mood for conversation. I am going

out to find some congenial company.' His eyes raked her dismissively. 'God knows it will not be difficult.'

She flinched inwardly. 'Please listen to me.'

'No, Katharina. We have already said everything that is necessary to each other.'

She lifted her chin. 'I've changed my mind.'

He was very still. 'In what way?'

'I can't go back with you,' she said rapidly. 'I won't.'

'Your rebellion is too late, *matia mou*. I shall not permit you to back out now.'

'You can't make me.' The words were uttered before she had time to think. And they were a mistake. She knew that even before she saw him smile.

'You don't think so? I say you are wrong, my wife.' He tossed his jacket on to a sofa. Took a step towards her.

'Perhaps I shall stay here after all, and show you that I can—persuade you to do anything I want. That I can take from you anything I desire, and you will let me. Because—still—you cannot help yourself. And you know it.'

He paused, letting the words sink in. 'Or would you prefer to stick to the bargain we have made after all—and spend your nights alone?'

'Yes,' she said. She kept her voice level, even though she was shaking inside. 'Yes, I would—prefer that.'

'You are wise.' His voice was mocking, as he retrieved his coat and shrugged it on. The dark eyes were hard. 'It has been a long time since I touched you, *agapi mou*, and almost certainly I would not have been gentle.'

He watched the colour drain from her face and nodded. He added courteously, 'I wish you a pleasant evening,' and went.

CHAPTER NINE

AS THE plane began its descent to Kefalonia airport, Kate broke the silence she'd maintained throughout the flight.

'The divorce.' Her voice was constricted. 'Have you really told—no one? Not even Iorgos Vasso?'

He would not have to tell Victorine, she thought. Because she already knew…

'No one.' Mick's tone was uncompromising, his eyes cold as he turned to look at her. 'And I intend it to remain a private matter between us, for the present, anyway. I do not wish to spoil a happy time for my sister.'

She bit her lip. 'You're all heart.'

He sighed. 'However if that is your attitude, we will deceive no one. And you will have reneged on our bargain.'

'God forbid,' Kate said bitterly. 'Don't worry, *kyrie*, I'll play the dutiful wife—in public at least.'

He said, 'It will also be necessary for us to exchange a few remarks from time to time—in public at least,' he added drily.

She lifted her chin. 'I'll do that too—if I must.'

'A small price to pay for freedom, surely?'

Oh, no, she thought, pain closing her throat. It's going to cost me everything.

The days they'd spent together in London had been almost more than she could bear. Not that they'd been together in any real sense, she reminded herself. Mick had been scrupulous about keeping his distance. During the daytime, he'd been in meetings, and she tried not to think where he could be spending his evenings and the greater part of each night. Clearly fidelity, even to Victorine, had never been on his agenda.

They deserve each other, she thought wrenchingly.

Yet, at the same time, all she knew was that she lay alone in the darkness, unable to sleep, straining her ears for the sound of his return.

And that, of course, was madness.

She had little to fill her days either. Iorgos Vasso had dealt with her employers, agreeing an extended and unpaid leave of absence, rather than the notice that Mick had advocated. He'd also arranged with an astonished Mrs Thursgood to have Kate's flat kept an eye on, and her mail forwarded.

The life she'd begun laboriously to assemble was being smoothly erased, she realised helplessly, and when she came back from Kefalonia, finally alone, she would have to rebuild it all over again.

Although that, at least, would give her something to think about, which she suspected she might need.

In accordance with Mick's instructions, she'd trawled reluctantly round Bond Street and Knightsbridge and bought some new clothes, more in keeping with her role as Mrs Theodakis, but she'd kept her expenditure to an absolute minimum.

And she would bring none of them back with her when she left. Her Kate Dennison gear was safely stowed in the bottom of one of her cases, waiting for this nightmare to be over.

The drive to the villa seemed to take no time at all. She had wanted time to compose herself for the ordeal ahead—to resist the ache of familiarity in the landmarks they were passing. To fight to the death the sense of homecoming that had assailed her as soon as the plane touched down.

The staff were clearly delighted to have her back. She was greeted with beaming smiles on all sides, and conducted ceremoniously indoors.

I feel a traitor, she thought angrily.

Her father-in-law was in the *saloni* glancing through some

papers, but he rose as Kate walked in and welcomed her with a swift, formal embrace.

'It is good to see you.' He stepped back, and looked at her critically. 'But you are thinner. This will not do.' He glanced at Mick. 'You will have to take better care of her, my son.'

'I intend to,' Mick returned, unsmilingly.

'I was worried when you went without saying goodbye.' Ari indicated that Kate should sit beside him. 'But Michalis told me it was an emergency. That you had been called away urgently.' He paused, eyeing her shrewdly. 'I hope it is all resolved now.'

She mustered a taut smile. 'Well—nearly, I think.'

'Perhaps we could have helped,' Ari suggested. 'We have teams of lawyers—accountants—business advisers—all with too little to do. Did Michalis not explain this?'

Kate bit her lip. 'It was a—private matter. I didn't want to trouble anyone else.'

'You are a Theodakis now, Katharina.' Ari patted her hand. 'Your problems are ours. But, you will be tired after the flight. Michalis, take her down to the beach house, and see that she rests.'

Kate's heart was thumping as she walked beside Mick down the track through the pine woods. How many times had she taken this same path with him, she wondered, knowing their bed and his arms awaited her?

And now she was on her way to pain, betrayal and deception. Just as she had been only a few short weeks before.

She stumbled on a loose stone, and he caught her arm, steadying her.

She wrenched herself free, glaring at him. 'Don't touch me. Don't dare.'

There was a shocked pause, then he said bleakly, 'You would rather fall than have me catch you. I understand.'

For a moment there was an odd expression on his face— bewildered. Almost—lost.

He still can't believe he isn't irresistible, Kate thought, lashing herself into fresh anger.

The house was just as she remembered it, with its faded terracotta tiles, and white walls festooned with flowering plants.

There were flowers inside, too, she discovered dazedly. In the master bedroom, every surface was covered by bowls full of blossoms. Like some bridal bower, she thought, checking in the doorway, faint nausea rising within her, as she looked across at the bed and remembered...

Saw her luggage standing in the corner.

She turned on Mick, standing silently behind her, her voice was harsh, strained. 'No—not this room. I won't stay here. Please have my things put in the other bedroom.'

His brows snapped together. 'I have been using that myself.'

'Then you'll have to change,' she flung at him.

You sleep in here. You live with the memories. Because I won't. I can't.

'If not, I'm leaving,' she went on recklessly. 'Going back to England, and to hell with our deal. To hell with everything. And if it blows your whole scheme out of the water—tough. But there's no way I'm going to sleep in that bed ever again.'

His face looked grey. He said hoarsely, 'Katharina—how in the name of God did we come to this?'

'Ask yourself that, *kyrie*.' Her voice was like stone. 'I'm just passing through.'

She went past him and walked the few yards down the passage to the second bedroom. The queen-size bed had clearly been freshly made up with clean sheets, and she sank down on its edge aware that her legs were shaking.

Mick followed. He said quietly, 'I have left a few things in the closet. I'll take them.'

'Yes,' she said. 'Then I can do my own unpacking.'

'Soula will do that, as usual.' He paused. 'And your clothes will stay in the other room—with me.'

'No.' Kate got to her feet. 'You can't do that.'

'You came here to preserve the illusion that we still have a marriage.' His voice bit. 'Most couples share a room—a bed. I ask you only to share a wardrobe. You may sleep where you please, *pedhi mou*. The night brings its own privacy.'

She bit her lip. 'Very well. Then I'll try and choose everything I need for the day each morning. At other times, I—I'll keep out of your way.'

There was silence, then he said very softly, 'I do not know if I can bear this.' And went.

Kate stood in the middle of the room, her arms wrapped round her body, until she stopped shaking. She felt bone-weary, but she knew that if she lay down, she would not be able to relax.

But it was still very warm for late September, so perhaps she would sit by the pool—or even go for a swim.

Her bathing suits were all in the master bedroom, she realised without pleasure. She went quietly along the passage, and knocked on the half-open door, but Mick was nowhere to be seen, so she went in.

The scent of the flowers was almost overwhelming as she searched for her black bikini.

As she retrieved it, and the pretty black and white overshirt that accompanied it, she heard swift footsteps approaching, and, a moment later, Ismene flung herself at her.

'Kate *mou*, at last. Oh, I am so happy you have come. I was so afraid you would not.' She pulled a face. 'Michalis made me send you the invitation. He said only when you saw it in black and white would you believe Papa had agreed.'

'What made him change his mind?' Kate shook her head. 'He seemed so adamant.'

Ismene shrugged, her expression puzzled. 'I do not know. He talked very strangely to me. Said how few people found the one person in the world who could make them happy,

and what right had he to deny me when Michalis had you, and he himself had loved Mama so much.'

She lowered her voice confidentially. 'Do you think he is growing tired of Victorine, perhaps? Wouldn't it be wonderful if he sent her away?'

Kate forced a smile. 'I—wouldn't count on it.'

'Anyway, what of you, sister?' Ismene went on, after a pause. 'Why did you leave like that—without even saying goodbye, *po, po, po*?'

'It was an emergency,' Kate said steadily, falling back on the agreed story. 'A family thing. I—I can't really discuss it.'

'But all is well now, and you will be staying here?'

Kate forced a smile. 'Nothing is certain in this uncertain world,' she said. 'But I'll definitely be here to see you married.'

'My dress is wonderful,' Ismene confided. 'Silk organza, and the veil my mother wore. Petros and I will marry in the morning at our village church, and then there will be a celebration in the square. And at night there will be a party here with dancing.' She sighed. 'But I shall miss most of that because I shall be on my honeymoon.'

Kate laughed in spite of herself. 'A honeymoon is far better than any party, believe me.'

Ismene eyed her speculatively. 'You and Michalis—did you do it *every* night?'

Kate gasped, feeling a wave of heat swamp her face, as she searched vainly for a reply.

Mick said from the doorway, 'That is none of your business, Ismene *mou*.' He strolled into the room, his face expressionless as he surveyed his wife's embarrassment. 'And if you make my Kate blush again, I shall tell Petros to beat you.'

She sent him a mischievous look. 'Perhaps I should enjoy that. But I can tell when I am no longer wanted,' she added with a giggle. 'I will see you later, Katharina.'

And she flew off again, leaving husband and wife facing each other.

Kate's face was still burning. She said, 'I—I thought I'd sit by the pool.'

He glanced at the bikini, dangling from her hand, and his mouth curled. 'Then I will use the beach.'

She looked at the floor. 'Isn't that rather going to extremes?' she asked in a low voice. 'Surely we don't have to avoid each other to that extent.'

'Ah, but we do,' he said. 'I promise you, *agapi mou*. You see, I still find the sight of you wearing next to nothing too disturbing to risk.' He began casually to unbutton his shirt. 'I am sure you understand.'

Kate sank her teeth into her lower lip. 'Yes,' she said. 'Yes, of course.' She remembered suddenly that the beach was Victorine's favourite haunt. 'But I'm sure you'll find an even more appealing view,' she added hastily, regretting it at once.

Mick tossed his shirt on the bed, and gave her a narrow-eyed look. 'What is that supposed to mean?'

She shrugged. 'Nothing. After all, you were the one who told me Kefalonia was a beautiful island.'

'But clearly not beautiful enough to tempt you to stay in our marriage.'

She stared at him in disbelief. 'You dare say that to me?' Her voice shook. 'When it was you—you...'

'You knew what I was when you met me.' Mick unbuckled his belt and unzipped his trousers. 'I never pretended that I could give you my undivided attention.'

'Am I supposed to admire your honesty?' Kate asked bitterly.

'I would have settled for acceptance.' He slipped his discarded trousers on to a hanger, put them in the closet, then walked over to her. 'Have you forgotten all the happy hours we spent in this room, *matia mou*.' His voice sank huskily. 'Is my sin really so impossible to forgive?'

It occurred to her suddenly that he was wearing nothing but a pair of his favourite silk shorts. Her throat tightened, and, flurried, she took a step backwards.

'Don't run away, Katharina *mou*.' He spoke softly, seductively. 'And don't you fight me any more. Stay with me now. Let me make amends to you. Show you how much I need you.'

His hands were gentle on her shoulders, drawing her close.

For a crazy moment, she found herself remembering how long it was since she'd really touched him. Since she'd let her fingers stray over his naked skin, tracing the steel of bone and muscle. Since her lips had adored the planes and angles of his lean, responsive body.

She wanted to run her fingers along the line of his shoulder, and kiss the heated pulse in his throat. She was hungry— frantic to feel the maleness of him lifting gloriously to her caress.

And then as if a light clicked on in her head, she remembered, and pulled herself free.

'Don't touch me,' she said between her teeth. 'Oh God, I should have known I couldn't trust you.'

Something flickered momentarily in his eyes, then he laughed curtly. 'You have a short memory, dear wife. This is my room—you were quite insistent about it. And I did not invite you here. You came of your own free will. You watched me undress.' He shrugged, his mouth twisting. 'It could be thought you were sending me a signal.'

'Then think again,' Kate flashed stormily. 'Do you seriously think that an—afternoon romp with you could repair the damage between us? And in this of all places.' She drew a harsh shuddering breath. 'Oh, God, I despise you. I hate you.'

He said quietly, 'I am beginning to understand that. I confess that I thought a—romp could be a start for us. A new beginning. But I see now that there is no hope.'

He paused. 'I will tell Soula to take all your clothing and

belongings to your own room after all. Then you need never set foot in here again.' He turned away. 'Now go.'

All Kate really wanted to do was crawl into her room, and hide in some dark corner while she licked her wounds.

But that was impossible. Even though she was dying inside, she had to salvage her pride—to pretend she didn't care. That Michael no longer had the power to hurt her.

She'd said she was going to spend some time by the pool, and that she would do, she resolved, straightening shoulders that ached with tension. Even if it killed her.

She stripped, and put on her bikini. The golden tan which she'd acquired earlier in the summer still lingered, she thought, subjecting herself to a critical scrutiny in the long wall mirror.

But, she was still losing weight. When she'd married Michael, her figure had been nicely rounded in all the right places. Now she could count the bones in her ribcage.

But, even at her best, she'd never come near Victorine's sinuously voluptuous quality, she thought, biting into her lower lip.

And her performance in bed would never match the sultry Creole's either.

That was a painful truth she could not avoid.

She was married to a passionate, experienced man, who had taken her for his own reasons. And, for him, the gift of her loving heart would never have been enough.

He wanted more, she thought. The kind of sophisticated playmate he'd been accustomed to in the past. Something she could never be.

Of course, he'd been endlessly patient with her in those first months, but, however willing the pupil, it was probably inevitable that he'd become bored with being the teacher. And the novelty had worn off for him long ago.

But that didn't mean she would ever accede to his cynical suggestion that she go along with this smokescreen marriage

she'd been tricked into. Turn a blind eye to his amours for the prestige of being Mrs Michael Theodakis.

She felt tears prick at her eyelids, and fought them back.

This might be the norm for marriage in the circles Michael Theodakis moved in, but it would never do for her. She cared too much, which no doubt rendered her doubly unfashionable. And no amount of money or luxury was going to change a thing.

Sighing, she trailed out into the sunshine.

It might be the day from hell, she thought, unhappily, as she adjusted the umbrella over her lounger and stretched out on the cushions, but there was still the evening, with the inevitable family dinner to endure somehow.

And Victorine…

There hadn't been a glimpse of her so far, or a mention, but Kate knew the other woman would simply be biding her time, waiting for the most destructive moment. She shivered. The sun was still warm, but the memory of that other hot, golden day hung over her like a shadow, impossible to dispel.

She'd run down through the pines that day with wings on her feet, on fire to see Mick—to throw herself into his arms and resolve the differences that had caused them to part in anger.

She'd been stupid to make the matter of her travelling with him into an issue. She should have been persuasive rather than confrontational. But when she realised that he meant what he said, and she was not going with him to New York, she'd simply lost her temper.

'I'm not some submissive wife,' she'd hurled at him. 'You can't just dump me in any convenient backwater while you go off roaming the world.'

'My work involves travel,' Mick snapped back. 'You know this. You have always known it, so why the fuss?'

'Because we're married, and I want to be with you—not spending my life alone in some different part of the universe.

I'm your partner, Mick, not your housekeeper. Or your mother,' she added recklessly.

And because we were happy in New York, she thought. Because we were by ourselves with no family around—or memories of the past...

His face closed. 'We will leave my mother out of the discussion, if you please. She was content with her life.'

'Was she?' Kate asked bitterly. 'I'd like to have her ruling on that. Just because she knew her place, it doesn't follow she was happy with it.'

The dark brows drew together. 'You go too far, my girl. And you would be alone anyway on this trip. I have already told you I would have no time to give you, or your reproaches, when you tell me that you're bored,' he added bitingly.

'I presume you'd be coming home to sleep at some point?' Kate glared at him. 'I'd be with you then. Or is that the problem?' she went on recklessly. 'Are you not planning to spend all your nights in the same bed, *kyrie*? Is that why you don't want me with you—because I might cramp your style?'

His face was like stone. 'Now you are being ridiculous,' he said harshly. 'And insulting. I have given you my reasons. Let that be the end of it.'

She said shakily, 'Don't tempt me...'

Her words dropped like stones into the taut silence.

Mick sighed. 'Katharina *mou*, I swear I will be back before you know it.'

'Oh, please.' Her voice radiated scorn. 'Don't hurry back on my account.'

That night, when he tried to take her in his arms, she'd turned away from him. 'I have a headache.'

There was a silence, then he said coldly, 'That is a lie, and we both know it. But let it be as you wish. I will not plead.'

And when she'd woken the next morning, he'd gone.

'Kyrios Michalis told us that you were unwell, *kyria*,'

Soula said, her forehead wrinkled with concern. 'And that we were to let you sleep.'

She said quietly, 'That was—considerate of him.'

But she couldn't fool herself. Not for a minute. For the first time, she and Mick had parted in anger and silence, and it hurt.

Nor was it any consolation to remind herself that it wasn't just a tiff, but a matter of principle.

I didn't handle it well, she told herself ruefully. And the headache thing was just stupid. All I've done is deprive myself of some beautiful memories to help me through his absence.

She sighed.

She'd have to make sure his welcome home was just perfect, which shouldn't be too difficult—especially if he was missing her as much as she was already longing for him.

As soon as he calls, she thought, I'll tell him so. Put things right between us.

But the first time he telephoned, she was visiting Linda.

'He was sorry to have missed you, *pedhi mou*,' Ari told her, and Kate made a secret resolve to stay round the villa and await his next call, however long it took.

But this plan misfired too, for, a few evenings later, her father-in-law informed her that Mick had telephoned during the afternoon.

'Why did no one ring me at the beach house?' she protested. 'I've been there all day.'

'It was only a brief call,' Ari said soothingly. 'And I thought also you had gone to Argostoli.'

She caught a glimpse of Victorine's catlike smile, and knew exactly who had sown that little piece of misinformation.

She managed a casual, smiling shrug. 'Ah well, better luck next time.'

But she wouldn't trust to luck, she decided grimly. Not with a joker like Victorine in the pack. She would phone

their New York apartment herself. But her calls were fruitless, because, as he'd predicted, he was never there.

And in spite of herself, she could not help wondering where he was—and who he might be with...

'You're looking a little ragged round the edges, honey,' Linda told her critically one day.

'Is that all?' Kate forced a smile. 'According to Victorine, I've lost what few looks I ever possessed. Not a day goes by without some snide remark,' she added smboulderingly.

Linda sighed. 'The woman is poison. Men can be so damned blind sometimes...' She paused. 'Anyway, Mick wouldn't want you to mope.'

Kate sighed. 'I'm not sure I know what Mick wants any more.'

'Theodakis men are never predictable.' Linda's tone was wry. 'It's part of their charm.'

She was silent for a moment. 'I'm going across to Ithaca tomorrow to collect some pots a friend of mine has made for me. Come with me.' Her eyes twinkled suddenly. 'After all, Ithaca's the island where Penelope waited all those years for Odysseus to come back. Maybe it'll put things in perspective for you.'

Kate smiled reluctantly. 'Not if I remember correctly some of the things Odysseus got up to on his travels. But I'd love to come.'

It would be good to get right away from the villa for a few hours, she thought. Ismene had relapsed into a slough of simmering discontent which made the atmosphere disagreeable enough without the addition of Victorine's softly-spoken jibes.

Much as she liked her father-in-law, he was no judge of women, she thought. Then paused, her heart thudding, as she remembered that Mick had been equally culpable in that particular respect.

After all, he chose her first, she thought, biting her lip.

'Come to the beach with me?' Ismene pleaded in an under-
tone at breakfast the next day. 'I need to talk to you, sister.
To ask your advice.'

'I can't, Ismene. I'm going to Ithaca with Linda.' Kate
said. She was faintly ashamed of her relief that she had a
get-out. Besides, she reminded herself, she had already given
Ismene the best possible advice many times—to be patient,
and to try not to antagonise her father any more.

She turned to Ari. 'I hope that's all right. I'll be back for
dinner.'

He waved an expansive hand. 'Enjoy your day, *pedhi mou*.
I shall not be here either. An old friend of mine is staying
near Skala, and we are going fishing together.' He looked at
Victorine who was crumbling a bread roll and looking exquisitely bored. 'Are you sure you will not come with us,
chrisaphi mou.'

Victorine shuddered elaborately. 'I'm sorry, *cher*, but I can
think of nothing worse. Except, perhaps, a trip to Ithaca,' she
added, flicking a derisive glance at Kate.

'Then it's fortunate we didn't invite you,' Kate said
sweetly, as she rose to her feet.

But, in the hallway, she was waylaid by Yannis. 'The telephone for you, *kyria*.'

Could it be Mick? Kate wondered, her heart lurching in
sudden excitement. She glanced at her watch, trying to work
out the time difference as she lifted the receiver, but it was
Linda's voice that reached her.

'Kate, honey, we're going to have to take a rain check on
the Ithaca thing. I'm starting a migraine, so I'll be out of
things for at least two days.'

'Oh, Linda, I'm so sorry. Is there anything I can do?'

'Not a thing.' Linda gave a weak chuckle. 'I just need to
lie down in the usual darkened room, and take my medica-
tion. I'll be in touch when I'm better.'

Kate replaced the receiver and stood irresolute for a moment. She could always stay at home, she supposed, but then

she was bound to be buttonholed by Ismene with another list of complaints about her father's tyranny, and she wasn't sure she could cope.

I have my own problems, she thought sighing.

And it might also be difficult to avoid Victorine, and the constant pinpricks she liked to inflict on Kate's already sensitised skin.

So she would use her day of freedom to go for a drive, she decided. To revisit some of the places Mick had shown her in happier times. And, to try and get her head together.

The holiday season was in full swing now, so she avoided the usual tourist spots, and drove up into the Mount Enos national park. She left her car near the tourist pavilion, and walked up through the dark firs to the summit. There was no mist today, and she could see the neighbouring island of Zakynthos rising majestically out of the turquoise and azure sea, and, further to the east, the mountains of the Peleponnese.

The air was like spring water from a crystal glass. It was very still. No voices—just the faint sigh of the breeze in the clustering trees, and the distant drone of an aircraft making its descent.

She looked, up, shading her eyes, to track its progress, and suddenly Mick was there with her, his image so strong that she could have put out a hand and touched him.

The clustering islands blurred, and the iridescent glitter of the sea broke into tiny fragments as the tears came.

She whispered brokenly, 'Michalis *mou*.'

She knew in that moment that whatever their differences, however great the apparent difficulties, she would do anything to make her marriage work.

Mick would never fit some Identikit New Man pattern of the ideal husband. In spite of his cosmopolitan background, he was too fiercely Greek for that. But, if he beckoned, she would walk through fire for him, and that was all that really mattered.

There would have to be adjustments, and these would need to be mutual, because she was no doormat, but she felt more at peace, and more hopeful than she had done for weeks.

She drove down with care to the main road, and turned north. She had a leisurely stroll along the beautiful Myrtos beach, then drove on to Assos for a seafood lunch.

When she got back to the villa, she decided as she drank her coffee, she would get on the phone to New York, and stay on it until she'd spoken to Mick, and told him she loved him. She'd call the apartment, the office—even his favourite restaurant if she had to, but she'd find him.

Or, she would take the first flight she could get to America and tell him in person.

I'll get Yannis to call the airline, she thought in sudden excitement. He can make me a reservation. And I'll do it now.

There was a telephone in the taverna, but, before she could tell Yannis what she was planning, he had burst into excited speech. 'Kyria Katharina, it is so good that you have rung. Because Kyrios Michalis is here. He returned two hours ago. He asked for you, and I told him you had gone to Ithaca.'

'That didn't happen, Yannis. I'm at Assos instead, and I'm coming straight back. But please don't tell him. I want to surprise him.'

'You are coming back from Assos, and you wish to make it a surprise, *kyria*,' he repeated, and she knew he was smiling. 'I understand. I will say nothing.'

As she drove back, she remembered the aircraft she'd heard on the mountain—the certainty that Mick was with her.

I must have sensed that was his plane, she thought wonderingly.

She'd been in such a hurry to see Mick, she'd left the keys in the car, hurtling recklessly down the track to the beach house.

She was breathless, laughing as she'd opened the bedroom door. And seen, in one frozen, devastating moment, the end

of her marriage, and the ruin of her happiness. The death of faith and trust. The total destruction of every cherished hope and dream she'd ever had.

Or ever would have.

Because until she could stop loving Mick, cut him out of her heart and mind forever, she would be unable to move on.

And she knew now, with a terrible certainty, that, in spite of what he'd done, it wasn't over yet.

Because nothing had changed, she thought despairingly. This was the truth she had to face.

That, God help her, she was doomed to love him for all eternity.

CHAPTER TEN

KATE wrapped her arms round her body, stifling the involuntary moan of pain forcing its way to her lips as she remembered Victorine's mocking smile, and the way she'd allowed the encircling towel to slip down from her bare breasts.

How she'd glanced at the bed, where Mick lay face down, his naked body totally relaxed in sexual exhaustion, as if to silently emphasise the totality of the betrayal.

Of course, I was supposed to be on Ithaca, Kate thought. And Ari was out on his friend's boat. They must have thought they were safe—that it was the perfect opportunity.

But how many times before that? How many snatched hours had there been?

There was Athens, of course. Victorine had practically flaunted that red flag in front of her.

So many signs. So many signals that she'd been too naïve—too trusting—too damned stupid to pick up.

She bit into her lip. The earthquake of realisation might be over, but the aftershock still lingered. The agony of accepting that her marriage had only ever been a cynical charade to conceal Mick's secret passion for his father's woman—the flamboyant, sensual beauty he had never ceased to want.

There was no one she thought bitterly, whom he would not betray in his pursuit of Victorine.

But he would not consider that he'd short-changed his convenient wife in any way. After all, she'd had his name, his money, and sex on demand—she would no longer call it love-making—so what more could she possibly want?

I wanted love, she thought achingly. The one thing he never offered.

Had it never occurred to either of them that she might carry her pain and shock to Aristotle Theodakis? That this reckless, forbidden passion might have robbed Mick of his other major ambition—to rule the Theodakis empire?

Or had he counted on Kate's innate sense of decency to keep him safe? The knowledge that she would not willingly involve anyone else in her suffering—especially the father-in-law who had treated her with such unfailing kindness?

But then Mick liked to take chances—in his business as well as his personal life. For him, that would have been just one more justified risk.

Like bringing her back here...

Her throat was dry and aching. She got up from the lounger, and trailed wearily into the house. She needed a cool drink.

In the kitchen refrigerator she found a tall jug of fresh lemonade, and she filled a tumbler, and added ice cubes.

She'd just taken a long, grateful swallow, when she heard footsteps approaching quickly along the tiled hallway and Victorine appeared in the doorway. She was wearing a brief white skirt, and a low-cut silk top in her favourite deep pink.

'So.' Her voice had a metallic ring. 'You came back. I did not think it possible.'

'Well, don't worry.' Kate replaced her glass with care on the counter top, aware that her hand was shaking. But she kept her voice steady, and her glance level. 'It's only a short visit. I'll be gone soon—permanently.'

Victorine hunched a shoulder, her gaze inimical. 'What have I to worry me? I am merely astonished you have so little pride that you return here.'

'I came for Ismene's sake, and at her invitation. No other reason.' Kate lifted her chin. 'But there is one thing. While I am here, you will not set foot in this house again. You and Michael must find some other corner to pursue your sordid little affair. Do I make myself clear?'

Victorine shrugged gracefully. 'As crystal, *chère*. But it

makes little difference.' She gave Kate a cat-like smile. 'We can wait. Anticipation can be—most exciting, don't you find?'

'Why yes,' Kate said calmly. 'For instance, I can hardly wait to get out of here, and leave this whole squalid situation behind me.'

Victorine laughed, her eyes hard. 'You are being very sensible. No scenes. No whining. Be sure that Michalis will pay generously for your discretion.'

No, thought Kate. I'm the one who'll pay. For the rest of my life.

Her voice was cool and clipped. 'Kindly go now, Victorine, and stay away from me. Or I might change my mind, and blow the whole thing out of the water.'

She retrieved her glass, and moved towards the window, deliberately turning her back on her adversary and, after a moment, she heard the receding click of her heels as the other woman retreated.

She leaned against the wall, her shoulders sagging wearily, sudden tears thick in her throat. She'd won the encounter, but it was a hollow victory.

But, if self-interest prompted the Creole girl to keep her distance, it might make Kate's enforced stay on Kefalonia marginally more bearable.

Certainly, it was the best she could hope for.

She glimpsed her reflection in the window, the white strained face, the over-bright eyes, and trembling mouth.

And thought, 'You fool. Oh, God, you pathetic fool.'

She took a long, warm bath, then lay on her bed, with the shutters closed, and tried to sleep. To stop her brain treading the same unhappy paths all over again.

Selective amnesia, she thought, staring into the shadows. That was what she needed. The events of the past year painlessly removed from the memory banks.

And if she'd only obeyed her instincts and not gone to the

Zycos Regina with Lisa that night, she would never have met Mick, and none of this would have happened.

When she eventually dozed, she was assailed by brief troublous dreams, which left her tense and unrefreshed.

But she had no real reason to feel relaxed, she reminded herself ironically. She had the evening's family dinner to get through.

She pulled a straight skirt in sapphire-blue silk jersey from the wardrobe, and found the matching top, long-sleeved, and scooped neck.

She was brushing her hair, and trying to decide whether to sweep it up into a loose knot, or leave it unconfined on her shoulders, when there was a swift tap on the door and Mick walked in.

She swung round defensively. 'I didn't say "Come in."'

His smile did not reach his eyes. 'But I'm sure the words were hovering on your lips, *agapi mou*,' he drawled.

He placed a velvet covered case on the dressing table, and put a small Tiffany's box beside it.

'Your pendant,' he said. 'I would like you to wear it tonight.'

'And your orders naturally must be obeyed.'

He said quietly, 'I'd hoped you would look on it as a request, Katharina—but, so be it.'

She touched the other box. 'And this?'

'Some earrings to match it.' He paused. 'I brought them back from New York some weeks ago, but you were not here to receive them.'

Kate stiffened. 'Another attempt to salve your guilty conscience?' Her voice bit.

He was silent for a moment. 'What do you wish to hear? That I am not particularly proud of myself? I admit it.'

'Big of you to say so,' she said huskily. 'Only, it doesn't matter any more.'

'It matters to me.' He pushed the little box towards her. 'Please open your gift.'

'I prefer to regard it as an unwanted loan.' She had to stifle a gasp when the blue fire of the exquisite drops flared up at her from their velvet bed.

'Put them on,' Mick directed softly. Standing behind her, he buried both hands in the silky mass of her hair, and lifted it away from her ears, watching as Kate, summoning every scrap of self-control she possessed, fastened the tiny gold clips into her lobes.

'Beautiful.' He bent his head, letting his lips graze the smooth curve between throat and shoulder, his hand gently stroking the nape of her neck.

She felt a shiver run through her nerve-endings at his touch. Experienced the shock of need deep within her.

She looked down at her hands, clenched together in her lap, refusing to meet the compulsion of his dark gaze in the mirror.

She said in a stifled voice. 'Don't—touch me.'

There was a silence, then he straightened, moving unhurriedly, away from her.

He said mockingly, 'You have a saying, *matia mou*—that old habits die hard. I suspect it may be true for us both.'

A moment later, she heard the door close.

But when she emerged from her room, he was waiting for her.

'I regret the necessity.' He spoke curtly. 'But it will look better if we arrive together.'

'And we must never forget appearances.' She fiddled with the thin wool wrap she was wearing round her shoulders.

'But, of course not. Isn't that why you're here?'

And there was no answer to that, she reflected bitterly, as she walked up through the tall sighing pines, at his side.

The evening was not, however, as bad as she'd expected. Petros was there, with his parents whom she had never met before. Dr Alessou was a squarely built, grizzled man, and his wife was tall with a shy smile, and Kate liked them both

immediately. It was a pleasure to stand and talk to them, as well as a lifeline.

Linda was also present.

'Hi, stranger.' She gave Kate a swift hug. 'It's good to have you back.'

'Thank you.' Kate's smile was constrained, and Linda's brows drew together as she studied her.

'Come to lunch tomorrow,' she said. 'If Mick can bear to let you out of his sight.'

Kate straightened her shoulders determinedly. 'That's—not a problem.'

'Really?' Linda queried drily. 'I'll expect you at twelve.'

The only awkward moment came halfway through the meal, when Ismene, who was on bubbling form, spotted Kate's earrings.

'Are they to welcome you back?' she demanded breathlessly. 'How much he must have missed you, *po, po, po.*' She sent a laughing look at her silent brother. 'If I were Katharina, I would go away again and again. What will you bribe her home with next time, Michalis—a ring, perhaps, with a stone like a quail's egg?'

He was leaning back in his chair, out of the candlelight, so Kate could not see his expression. But his voice was cool even with a note of faint amusement. 'I am saving that, *pedhi mou*, until our first child is born.'

'What is this?' Ari barked jovially from the head of the table. 'Have you some news for us, my girl?'

'No.' Kate was burning from head to foot. Suddenly she was the focus of everyone's attention—genial, interested, excited—and, in one case, poisonous. She just wanted to get up from the table and run. 'No, of course not.'

'They are both young.' Dr Alessou looked at her kindly. 'There is plenty of time. Ari, my friend.'

'But times are changing.' Ari Theodakis looked round the table commandingly. 'I have reached a decision. At the next full meeting of the board, I shall officially announce my re-

tirement as chairman of the International Corporation. It is time I made way for new blood.'

He inclined his head towards Mick. 'I leave my companies in your safe hands, my son.'

There was an astonished silence.

'But what are you going to do, Papa?' Ismene was wide-eyed.

He smiled benignly. 'I have my plans. My friend Basilis Ionides has just completed the purchase of his property, which as you know includes the old Gianoli vineyard. We are going to restore its fortunes—make wine together. And I shall tend my olives, go fishing, and sit in the sunlight. And play with my grandchildren.' He grinned at Dr Alessou. 'I may also find time for the occasional game of *tavli*, eh, my friend?'

Kate still struggling to regain her composure saw Victorine's face turn to stone, indicating that Ari's announcement was news to her. She saw, too, the lightning glance that the other woman darted at Mick.

He's got what he wanted, she thought. And now he can have her too. Once he's officially chairman, there'll be nothing to stop him.

And Victorine likes the high life. She wants a millionaire not a Kefalonian farmer. Vines and olive groves will never be enough for her. Surely Ari must realise that.

But there won't be a thing he can do about it, once he's given up the reins. So, there'll be a ghastly scandal, the press will have a field day, and the family feud will break out all over again.

She looked down at the golden gleam of her wedding ring. And she would be bound to be dragged into it too—splashed across the newspapers as the wronged wife. Made to relive every bitter moment all over again. A far cry from the quiet divorce she'd planned.

But no one could hope to escape unscathed from this kind of situation, she reminded herself wretchedly. It was only

astonishing that no enterprising journalist had managed to dig out the facts about this sordid little love triangle a long time ago.

Or was it just proof of the influence the Theodakis family were able to wield, and the privacy their money had always succeeded in buying for them?

But it wasn't her problem. Not any longer. And in a few months she'd be free of it all, she told herself, sinking her teeth into her bottom lip. And her transient encounter with the rich and mighty would be eventually forgotten.

Although, not by her. That was too much to hope for.

She was sitting in her own little cocoon of silence amid the welter of laughter and surprised comment around the rest of the table when a slight prickle of awareness made her look up.

Mick was watching her across the table. He was frowning faintly, his face taut, the dark eyes concerned, and questioning.

Oh, please don't worry, she assured him silently, and bitterly. I won't rock the boat. Not at this juncture.

I'll run away again, as soon as Ismene's wedding is over, and you can tell your father I couldn't cope with the prospect of being the chairman's lady. That I simply wasn't up to it. The truth can wait for a more convenient moment—after the official announcement that you're the new chairman.

She drank some wine from her glass, then turned determinedly to Dr Alessou, an authority on island history, to ask a bread and butter question about St Gerassimos, who was Kefalonia's patron, and to whom the village church was dedicated.

He launched himself into his subject with enthusiasm, and when Kate next dared steal a glance under her lashes at Mick, she found he was talking with smiling courtesy to the doctor's wife.

*   *   *

The evening seemed endless, and wore the air of an occasion, thwarting any hopes Kate might have had of making an unobtrusive exit.

Especially when Yannis entered ceremoniously with champagne.

'A double celebration,' Ari explained. 'My retirement, and your return to us, *pedhi mou.*'

Kate smiled, and felt like Judas.

But at last the Alessous took their leave, and Kate felt free to escape too.

She said a general 'Goodnight,' but she had only gone a few yards down the moonlit track to the beach house, when Mick caught up with her.

'What do you want?' She faced him defensively.

'It's our first night here together,' he said. 'It would be thought odd if I did not accompany you.'

'It must be a relief to know that you won't have to keep up appearances for much longer.'

'So it seems.' His tone was wry. 'It came as quite a bombshell.'

'The first of many, I'm sure,' Kate said crisply, and set off down the track, shoulders rigid.

'And for that very reason, we need to talk, my Kate.'

She said unevenly, 'Don't call me that. And there's nothing more to discuss. We established the terms for my return in London. Nothing has changed.'

'You were very angry in London. I have been waiting—hoping that, perhaps, your temper had begun to cool.'

'I'm not angry, *kyrie.* I'd just like to get on with the rest of my life.' She paused, wrapping her arms defensively round her body, not looking at him. 'After all, you've just achieved your heart's desire.'

He said slowly, 'If you think that, *agapi mou*, then our marriage has taught you nothing.'

'Then it's as well it's over,' Kate returned curtly, and walked on.

He caught her arm, and spun her round, making her face

him in the moonlight. He said quietly, 'I do not—cannot believe you mean that, Kate. Not in your heart.'

'Fortunately I've started using my brain instead, *kyrie*. Something our marriage *has* taught me.' She tried to tug herself free. 'Now let go of me.'

'How easy you make that sound.' Mick's voice was bitter. 'But perhaps I am not ready to give up on us so easily, *matia mou.*'

She took a step backwards. 'You can say that.' Her voice shook. 'You *dare* to say that.'

'Katharina.' He sounded almost pleading. 'I know what I did was wrong, but is my fault really so unforgivable? Could we not—negotiate some new terms?'

What do you want from me? she cried silently. To go on with this charade—pretend we have a marriage? Enjoy the money and the prestige and turn a blind eye to your other pleasures? Because I can't. I can't...

She said tautly, 'That's impossible, and you know it.'

'I know nothing any more.' Mick's voice was harsh. 'Except that, for one stupid act, my life with you has been destroyed.'

'I was the stupid one,' Kate said bleakly. 'Thinking I could ever be content with the kind of half-life you had to offer.'

'*Agapi mou.*' There was real anguish in his tone. 'Believe me, I never meant to hurt you like this.'

No, she thought. Because I was never meant to find out. I was expected to stay the naïve innocent until you decided otherwise.

'Oh, my Kate.' His voice sank to a whisper. 'Even now, couldn't you find it in your heart to forgive me? Offer me another chance? We could be happy again...'

'No.' She began to walk down the track again. 'I'm not the same person. Not the blind idiot you married.'

She knew that note in his voice. It had always been the prelude to lovemaking. And she had always responded to it.

He was still holding her arm, as he walked beside her, and

she felt his touch through the silky sleeve, scorching her flesh, burning her to the bone. She was falling to pieces, suddenly, blind and shaking. Her reason fragmenting.

And soon—all too soon—they would reach the house where the lamps would have been lit in their absence, and the wide bed in the main bedroom turned down in readiness, just as always.

That room, where the pale drapes shimmered in the breeze through the shutters, and the moonlight dappled the floor.

Where she heard her name whispered in the darkness and opened her arms to him in joy and welcome.

That was how it had been only a few short weeks before.

And how it could never be again.

That was the truth—the rock she had to cling to as emotion and stark need threatened to overwhelm her.

'I've changed too, *agapi mou.*' His voice reached her softly, pleadingly. 'Surely—surely that could be a start—a way for us to find each other again.'

'You said you wouldn't do this,' Kate accused raggedly. 'Oh, why the hell did I come back here? Why did I ever trust you?'

'Did you really believe I would just let you walk away?' Mick followed her into the dimly lit hallway. 'And I said I would allow you to sleep alone—not that I wouldn't fight to get you back.'

'Well the battle's over, *kyrie.*' She wrenched herself free from his detaining hand. 'And you lost.'

'Are you so sure?' he asked quietly. His eyes went over her, registering the widening eyes, the tremulous parted lips, and the uncontrollable hurry of her breathing.

He moved towards her, and she took a swift step backwards only to find further retreat blocked by the wall behind her.

Slowly and deliberately, he rested his hands against the wall on either side of her, holding himself at arm's length,

not touching her in any way, but keeping her trapped there just the same.

Over his shoulder, she could see the half open door of his bedroom. All the flowers had been removed, but their scent still seemed to hang in the air, sweet and evocative.

'Shall I show you that there are no certainties between a man and a woman, *matia mou*—just an infinite range of possibilities?' There was a note of shaken laughter in his voice. 'Won't you let me make amends for the past?'

Kate lifted her chin, making herself meet the power—the unconcealed hunger of his dark gaze with white-faced defiance.

'What are you suggesting, *kyrie*—that we should solve everything by having sex?'

His brows lifted 'It might at least provide a beginning—a way back. And I had hoped that we would make love to each other,' he added with cool emphasis.

Kate shrugged. 'Dress it up however you want. It comes to the same thing in the end.'

'No,' he said with sudden bitterness. 'It does not, my innocent wife.' He looked down at her, his mouth tightening harshly. 'Do you wish me to demonstrate.'

'No.' Her voice was a thread.

He sighed. 'Don't fight me any more, Kate *mou*.' His voice gentled. 'Because I could—make you want me, and you know that.'

'Not any more.' She crossed her arms defensively over her breasts—a gesture that was not lost on him. 'Understand this, Michael. Whatever you did to me, whatever you called it, it would be nothing more than rape. And I'm sure you don't want that on what passes for your conscience.'

His head went back as if she had struck him across the face.

He said hoarsely, 'Kate—you do not—you cannot mean this. In the name of God, you are my wife.'

'Only in the eyes of the law,' Kate said. 'And even that will change soon.' She swallowed. 'Now let me go.'

There was a long, tingling silence. She saw the incredulity in his eyes fade and become replaced by something infinitely more disturbing—even calculating. A look that sent a shiver curling through her body.

Then Mick straightened slowly, almost insolently, his arms dropping to his sides.

So that technically she was free. And all she had to do was turn and walk away. Only she couldn't seem to move—leave the support of the wall, or the ice-cold compulsion of his gaze.

He said too softly, 'So—what are you waiting for. To be wished a restful night, or, perhaps—this?'

There was not even time for a heartbeat. Suddenly, Kate was in his arms, crushed without gentleness against his lean body, her parted trembling lips being plundered by his.

There was no tenderness in the kiss he subjected her to. Just a ruthless, almost cold-blooded sensuality that bordered on punishment.

Her first faint moan of protest was smothered by the bruising pressure of his mouth. After that, she was incapable of speech or even thought. Even to breathe was a difficulty. But there was no mercy in the arms that held her, or the hard lips that moved on hers with almost brutal insistence.

Behind her closed eyelids, fireflies swirled in a frantic, mocking dance.

In spite of herself, her starved body was awakening to stinging, passionate life under the searing shock of his kiss. The scent, the taste of him filled her nose and mouth with a frightening familiarity. The awareness that he was strongly starkly aroused sent swift heat coursing through her veins, and awoke memories as potent as they were unwelcome.

Her head was reeling. Her legs were shaking under her. She was going to faint. She might even die. But nothing

mattered except the urgent, agonised necessity of feeling the burning strength of him inside her, filling her.

She pressed herself against him, letting the wild current of feeling carry her away to recklessness.

Later, she would be ashamed. Would hate herself.

But tonight, for a few brief hours, he would belong to her alone. An encounter to treasure in the loneliness ahead.

And in that instant she found herself free, her release as sudden and startling as a blow. Mick stepped backwards, away from her, studying her through narrowed eyes, as he fought his own ragged breathing.

Kate sagged back against the wall, staring back at him, her wide eyes clouded with desire, a hand pressed to her swollen mouth as she waited.

Waited for him to lift her into his arms, and carry her to bed. Waited to feel his mouth on hers again, demanding the response she longed to give.

He was close enough to touch, yet the distance between them had suddenly become a vast and echoing space, impossible to bridge.

And his smile, she saw, was cold, and faintly mocking.

Swift dread invaded her, like a sliver of ice penetrating her heart.

'*Kalinichta, matia mou,*' he drawled. 'Goodnight—and I wish you sweet dreams. As sweet as that night on Zycos, perhaps.'

She watched him walk away from her across the passage, and heard the finality of his door closing.

Shutting her out. Leaving her in a limbo of her own making, composed of shame and regret.

CHAPTER ELEVEN

IT WAS a long time before Kate could move. Before she could find the strength to walk, stumbling a little, the few yards to her own room.

She closed the door with infinite care, then trod across the room to the bed. She sat on its edge, hands clenched in her lap in a vain attempt to stop them shaking.

She'd made him angry. That was the only logical explanation for the last shattering minutes. She'd refused to be manipulated. To allow herself to be used.

Because that was all it was, she told herself. He couldn't risk a rendezvous with his mistress, and he needed a woman. So, why not amuse himself by seducing his gullible wife all over again?

Kate winced as her teeth grazed the tender fullness of her lower lip.

Perhaps he'd thought again about the public resumption of his liaison with Victorine, recognising it as the kind of conduct the Theodakis board would condemn.

Or maybe he'd decided he needed the surface respectability of his current marriage after all, no matter what might happen in private.

The cynicism of it nauseated her.

But, that being the case, why hadn't she walked away from him, while she had the chance? What had induced her to stay, and provoke him into that storm of devastation that he'd unleashed on her.

It was madness—and, bitter as the acknowledgment might be, she only had herself to blame.

And why hadn't she fought him? she asked herself wildly.

She could have struggled—kicked—bitten. But she'd done none of those things.

She slipped off her shoes, and lay back on the bed in a small, defensive curve.

Because she hadn't wanted to, she thought. That was the next unpalatable truth she had to deal with.

However much her reason might condemn Mick, and affirm that she could not go on living with him after such a betrayal, her physical responses were operating on a different planet.

At his lightest touch, her body seemed to open, like a flower, creating that deep, molten ache which only he could heal. Even the thought of him could make her whole body clench in hunger and need.

None of the hurt, the anger and bitterness had managed to cure her of wanting him, and she was going to have to live with that.

But, which was far worse, Mick was totally aware of the war going on between her mind, and her too-eager senses, because he knew her better than she knew herself.

He'd pinpointed her weakness with mind-numbing brutality, leaving her without a hiding place, or even an excuse. And he'd done it quite deliberately.

He was also the one who had, in the end, walked away.

And, somehow, she had to survive the despair and humiliation of that knowledge, and go on.

When all she really wanted to was run ignominiously away.

Except that would be pointless, Kate thought, burying her face in the pillow. There could be no escape, because Mick had her on the end of some invisible chain, and all he had to do was tug, and she would be drawn back inexorably. And no amount of time or distance would change a thing.

And how was she going to live with that?

She cried for a while, then, silently, achingly. When there

were no more tears left, she sat up wearily, pushing back her hair from her face.

She took the diamonds from her ears and around her throat, and put them back in their cases, then undressed, and donned her simple white cotton nightshirt.

She had known from the beginning, she thought, as she lay in the darkness listening to the whisper of the sea, that she and Mick came from two different worlds. Yet in truth they were light years apart.

How could he regard such a transgression, such a complete betrayal, so lightly? she asked herself wretchedly. Unless he felt he was powerful enough to ignore the normal rules of morality.

He'd clearly expected her to shrug and smile, and take him back when he asked for forgiveness. Presumably that was how other wives of his acquaintance reacted to their husbands' passing adulteries.

But this was no trivial, transient affair, she reminded herself unhappily. No moment of weakness to be instantly regretted.

Because Victorine had clearly got into his blood. A habit he was unable to break. Maybe even a necessity…

Her mind closed at the thought.

Perhaps he even hoped that I'd be docile—besotted enough to accept some kind of *ménage à trois*, she thought bitterly.

She shivered, and turned over, trying to compose herself for sleep, but it would not come. Her mind was wide awake, endlessly turning on the treadmill of their last encounter.

Or perhaps she was just scared to sleep. Frightened in case the dreams that Mick had ironically wished for her might indeed be waiting to enclose her in their dark thrall, and draw her down to her own private hell.

It was nearly dawn when she at last closed her eyes, and only a few hours later when the sun woke her again, pouring through the slats in the shutters.

For a moment, she was tempted to stay where she was. To

pull the sheet over her head, and lie still, like a hunted animal gone to ground. Or even to feign illness.

But Ismene wanted her to talk about the wedding arrangements, she remembered, and she was also having lunch with Linda. Life was waiting for her, and could not be avoided.

It won't be for much longer, she told herself, as she bathed and dressed in her denim skirt and a simple white vest top. She hung small gold hoops in her ears, and used concealer to cover the shadows under her eyes, and blusher to soften her pallor.

She could hear the clash of crockery in the kitchen, and a woman's voice singing softly in Greek as she went through the living room, and out on to the terrace by the pool.

A table had been laid there, now littered with the remains of breakfast, and Mick was seated beside it, engrossed in some papers.

He was wearing shorts and a thin cotton shirt, open to the waist, and his hair was damp, indicating that he'd been swimming.

Kate paused, slipping her hands into the pockets of her skirt, and feeling them ball nervously into fists.

He glanced up at her hesitant approach, his gaze cool, almost dispassionate, with none of the mockery she'd feared.

He said, '*Kalimera*,' and pushed a small silver bell across the table towards her, as she took her seat. 'If you ring, Maria will bring you some fresh coffee and hot rolls.'

'Is that who was in the kitchen?' Kate frowned. 'Why is she here?'

'I decided it would be better if one of the servants was here to look after us.' His tone was expressionless.

'But I've always done that.' The words were out before she could stop herself.

'Ah, yes,' he said. 'But that was then. This is now.' His brief smile did not reach his eyes. 'And I have resolved, *matia mou*, to spare you *all* your wifely duties.'

She was aware that warm colour was staining her face, but kept her voice steady. 'I see.'

'But, of course, there are also the nights,' he went on. 'When Maria will not be here.' He paused. 'So, a man is coming from Argostoli this afternoon to put a lock on your bedroom door—in case my animal instincts should suddenly overwhelm me, you understand.'

'Please—don't…' Her voice was husky.

'Why not?' Mick shrugged. 'I am merely trying to simplify matters. To make your final days here as trouble free—and as safe—as I can. I thought you would be grateful.'

'Yes,' she said. 'You're—very considerate.'

'Thank you.' His mouth twisted. 'Perhaps we can maintain the normal courtesies, if nothing else.' He rose, stretching casually, causing Kate to avert her gaze rapidly from the long, tanned legs and the silken ripple of muscles across his bare chest and diaphragm.

'Now ring for your breakfast,' he added, putting his papers together. He offered her a quick, taut smile. 'I will not stay here to spoil your appetite.'

She wasn't hungry, but she made herself eat some of the rolls, honey and fresh fruit that Maria brought.

She might be sick at heart, she thought, but there was no point in making herself physically ill as well.

After all, the last thing she wanted was to look as if she was fading away under Victorine's gloating gaze.

'You do not look as if Michalis allowed you much sleep last night, sister,' was Ismene's exuberant greeting, when Kate joined her up at the villa. She gave her a wide smile. 'Life is good, *ne*?'

'Very good,' Kate returned, mentally crossing her fingers for the lie. And so much for cosmetic cover-ups, she added silently.

It was a relief to escape from her own problems into Ismene's joyful plans for her marriage.

Rather to Kate's surprise, the wedding was not to be some

glittering international event packed with the rich and famous.

The Theodakis clan was a vast one, and Petros also came from a large and widespread family. After that the guest list seemed restricted to old friends.

Most of the arrangements were already in place, largely thanks to Linda, Kate gathered. Her own task was largely one of room allocation at the villa, and booking accommodation in local hotels for the overflow.

As she'd suspected, Victorine's sole contribution had been a series of snide remarks about Ismene's marrying beneath her.

'But I told her that would never be her problem,' Ismene said with undisguised satisfaction. 'As there is no way down from the gutter.'

Kate choked back a laugh. 'Ismene—you could get into real trouble.'

'I thought so too,' Ismene admitted. 'But although she told Papa and he was stern with me, I do not believe he was really angry.' She gave Kate a hopeful look. 'Do you think he is becoming tired of her, Katharina? I could not bear it if she became my step-mother. And nor could Michalis.'

'No.' Kate's throat tightened. 'I—I'm sure he couldn't.' She hesitated. 'I think maybe we need to leave them to—work things out for themselves.'

But, perhaps, in the end, everyone would get what they wanted without scandal or an explosive rupture between Mick and his father, she thought later, as she drove down to Sami.

If Ari no longer wanted Victorine, he might not care too much if she was ultimately reunited with Mick. Father and son seemed to share a cynical view of women as commodities to be traded.

If only she herself could have been excluded from this sexual merry-go-round.

Yet, she knew in her heart that, in spite of betrayal and

heartbreak, she would not have missed the heady delights of those first months with Mick for anything in the world.

Although that was small consolation when she contemplated the empty desolation that awaited her.

'I thought we'd have lunch in the garden,' Linda said briskly, leading the way to her sheltered courtyard. 'While we still can. The weather's going to change,' she added, directing a critical look at the sky.

'How do you know?' Kate asked baffled.

'Live here for long enough, and you get the feeling for it.' Linda smiled at her. 'I bet Mick would tell you the same.'

'Yes.' Kate returned the smile with determination. 'Can you forecast whether we'll have a fine day for the wedding?'

'I can guarantee it.' Linda poured wine. 'The sun always shines on the Theodakis family. Haven't you noticed?' She paused as her maid brought bread and salad, and a platter of *crasato*—pork simmered in wine. So Kate was not forced to reply.

'Well,' Linda said when they were alone, and eating. 'What's the problem?'

Kate dabbed at her lips with the linen napkin. 'I don't know what you mean.'

Linda sighed. 'Honey—who are you kidding? You do not have the look of a girl in the throes of a blissful reunion with her man. And Mick looks as if he's strung up on wires, too. So, what's happening.'

Kate stabbed at her pork. 'I can't tell you. Not yet.'

Linda whistled, her face concerned. 'That bad, huh?' She was silent for a moment. 'I admit I wondered when you just disappeared like that. I planned to talk to Mick about it, if he'd let me, but he was never around long enough. Always working like a demon, rarely touching base. Which should have told me something, too,' she added thoughtfully.

'But when I heard he was bringing you back, I hoped that meant you'd managed to resolve your differences. God knows, there were bound to be plenty. You're both strong

characters. But so were Ari and Regina, and they rode out their storms. In fact, they thrived on them. I thought you'd be the same.'

Kate smiled over-brightly. 'I think that would rather depend on the storm.' She took some more salad. 'This food is delicious. And what herb has Hara used in the potatoes?'

Linda picked up the cue, and the conversation turned to food, and, from there, to the wedding.

'Have you decided what you're going to wear?' Linda asked.

Kate wrinkled her nose. 'Not really. I have this pale-green dress that Mi...that I bought back in New York. That's a possibility. But Ismene is talking of going to Athens shopping for a couple of days with Mrs Alessou,' she added. 'I could always go with them and find something there.'

They were just drinking their coffee, when they heard footsteps and Ari came round the corner of the house. He halted, brows lifting when he saw Kate.

'*Me sinhorite*. I beg your pardon, Linda. I did not realise you had a visitor. I should have knocked at your door and not taken it for granted that you could receive me.'

'Old friends never intrude,' Linda assured him, her face faintly flushed. 'Sit down, Ari, and have some coffee with us.'

'No, no, I was just passing, and I thought...' He sounded awkward. 'The vineyard I mentioned last night. I am going there now, and I wondered if you would care to come with me. But I see it is not possible. Another time, perhaps.'

'It's perfectly possible,' Kate said firmly, concealing her surprise. She pushed back her chair, and stood up. 'I was about to go, anyway. I have an ocean of things to do this afternoon.'

'You could always come with us, *pedhi mou*,' Ari suggested, with what Kate felt was real nobility.

She smiled and shook her head. 'Not today. Three's a

crowd, and always will be.' As I know only too well, she added under her breath, wincing.

'So,' she said mischievously, as Linda accompanied her out to her car. 'How long has this been going on?'

Linda's flush deepened. 'There's nothing "going on",' she responded with dignity. 'Just as I said, we are old friends. And he dropped by a couple of times while you were away to ask my advice about Ismene. That's all.'

Kate kissed her lightly. 'And now he wants to consult your expertise on winemaking. Fine.'

She was smiling to herself as she drove away. Maybe one good thing was going to emerge out of this unholy mess after all, she thought wistfully.

Although it would also mean that Mick was totally free to reclaim Victorine for himself. His trophy woman, she thought, as an aching sigh escaped her.

Within a few days, the countdown to the wedding had begun in earnest, leaving Kate little time for unhappy introspection. But, though her days might be full, her nights were another matter. Behind her locked door, she tossed and turned, searching vainly for peace and tranquillity.

Sharing the beach house with Mick was not easy, although she couldn't fault his behaviour. He was working hard, constantly away on short trips. But, when he was at home, he kept out of her way as much as possible, and, when they did meet, treated her with cool civility. Which, she supposed, was as much as she could hope for.

The weather had changed as prophesied, and rain fell from grey skies accompanied by a swirling wind. Without her usual escape routes through the pine woods, and to the beach, Kate began to feel almost claustrophobic, especially as nervous pressure began to build up at the villa with Ismene complaining that the village party would be ruined.

Even when money was no object, weddings were still tricky to arrange, Kate realised, as she dealt with tempera-

mental caterers, and found a replacement for the folk-dance troupe whose leading male dancer had broken his leg.

The shopping trip to Athens was a welcome break, with Ismene making heroic and endearing efforts to keep her spending within bounds, so as not to shock her future mother-in-law.

Kate had no need to set herself any such limits. She had been stunned to discover how much money was waiting in her personal account. It seemed that Mick had continued to pay her allowance during their separation. She couldn't fault his generosity in that regard, she thought, biting her lip.

And yet, in the end, she spent hardly anything. She trawled the boutiques and designer salons around Kolonaki Square with almost feverish energy, and tried on an astonishing array of garments to try and find an outfit for the wedding, but there was nothing that aroused more than a lukewarm interest in her.

In the past, when she'd gone clothes shopping, Mick had usually accompanied her. It had been fun to emerge from the changing room and parade breathlessly in front of him, waiting for him to signal approval or negation as he lounged in one of those spindly gilt chairs.

A nod was generally enough but, sometimes, she saw his attention sharpen, brows lifting, and mouth slanting in a smile as his eyes met hers, making her dizzyingly aware that he was anticipating the pleasure of taking off whatever expensive piece of nonsense she was wearing.

Now, it no longer mattered what she wore, she thought.

And she had the pale-green dress in reserve, she reminded herself. It was simple and elegant, and not overtly sexy, so it was suitable for a wedding, and, hopefully, would enable her to fade into the background during the day-long celebration.

But her restraint had not passed unnoticed.

'She tried on every dress in Athens,' Ismene reported teasingly on the evening of their return, when the family had

assembled in the *saloni* before dinner. 'And bought none of them. What do you think of that, Michalis?'

'Only that, for once, my prayers have been answered,' he returned wryly. Above the laughter, he added, 'And, anyway, I have my own ideas about what Kate should wear to your wedding, *pedhi mou*.'

'*Po, po, po.*' Ismene turned to Kate. 'What is he planning, do you suppose?'

'Who knows.' Kate made herself speak lightly. 'Your brother is good at surprises—and secrets.'

Her glance met his in unspoken challenge.

He said softly, 'And for that, *matia mou*, I shall make you wait until the day itself.'

As they went into the dining room, Kate found Victorine beside her.

'Your thrift is admirable, *chère*, and also wise.' The crimson mouth was smiling, as she whispered in Kate's ear. 'After all, one's financial circumstances can change so quickly, *n'est ce pas*? It is good to be prepared.'

Kate drew a sharp breath. 'I am more than ready, believe me,' she said icily, and turned away.

In spite of Ismene's gloomy forebodings, the clouds rolled away the day before the wedding, and a mellow sun appeared, bringing the island to life in shades of green and gold.

In twenty-four hours it will all be over, Kate thought bleakly. Ismene will be a wife—and I shall cease to be one.

A top hair stylist had come from Athens to attend to the bride, on the morning of the wedding, but Kate had declined his services. She already planned to wear her hair loose, with a small spray of cream roses instead of a hat.

But she still hadn't the least idea what dress Mick wished her to wear. The subject had not been referred to during any of their fleeting encounters, and she was damned if she was going to ask.

Let him be mysterious, she told herself, lifting her chin.

What difference does it make? It's just one more thing to endure on one more day from the rest of my life.

She had a leisurely bath, applied her favourite body lotion, and put on bra and briefs in ivory silk and lace, smoothing gossamer tights over her slim legs.

Holding her robe round her, she walked back into her bedroom, and checked, her lips parting in a little cry of shocked negation.

Lying across her bed was a slender slip of a dress in cream silk, cut on the bias so it would swirl around her as she moved, and beside it, its matching collarless jacket, the front panels embroidered with a delicate tracery of gold and silver flowers.

Her own wedding dress—worn only once before on that December day in London when all the happiness she'd ever dreamed of seemed to be within her grasp.

The last time she'd seen the dress, it had been hanging in her closet in the New York apartment.

He'd brought it back with him specially, she realised numbly. But why?

How could he hurt her like this? Why provide such a potent reminder of how things had once been between them, when they both knew their marriage was over? And that he was about to discard her forever?

She snatched up the folds of silk from the bed, and stormed down the passage to his room, rapping sharply at the closed door.

He called, '*Peraste*,' and Kate opened the door and marched in.

He was standing at the dressing table fastening his tie, but turned, brows raised, his gaze flicking her robed figure, and the dress hanging over her arm.

He said coolly, 'Is there a problem? Do you need help with your zipper perhaps?'

'No problem. I simply came to return this.' Kate con-

fronted him, chin lifted, allowing anger to mask her hurt and bewilderment. 'I won't wear it. You can't expect me to.'

He turned back to the mirror, making minute adjustments to the elegant knot at his throat.

'But I do expect it, Katharina *mou*,' he told her quietly. 'None of my family were at our wedding, so they have never seen you in that dress, or known how beautiful you looked. An omission I intend to rectify today.'

He paused. 'Besides, I told them last night what I was planning, so you cannot disappoint them. Such a romantic gesture to convince them all that we are the picture of marital harmony,' he added icily. 'Remember our bargain, and that you still have your part to play in it.' His smile was hard. 'Look on it as your costume for the last act, if you prefer. That might make it easier to bear.'

She said unevenly, 'I never thought you could be so cruel. Don't my feelings matter in all this?'

'Did you consider mine when you ran back to England?' he shot back at her. 'Without giving me a chance to explain—to apologise? Forcing me to invent stories to explain your absence.'

She said shakily, 'What you did was beyond apology. It would have been more honourable to have accepted responsibility and told the truth. But of course that might have jeopardised your ultimate ambition.'

'We are preparing for my sister's wedding,' Mick said flatly. 'Shall we discuss my ambitions at a more convenient moment?' He turned and confronted her, hands on lean hips, long legs sheathed in elegant charcoal pants, his crisp white shirt dazzling against his olive skin.

'Now go, and change,' he directed. 'Unless you wish me to dress you with my own hands,' he added significantly.

She took a step backwards. 'You wouldn't dare.'

'Don't tempt me, *agapi mou*.' His voice slowed to a drawl, blatantly sexy, almost amused. 'Or we might miss the wedding altogether. Now go.'

She gave him a fulminating glance, then turned and went out of his room back to her own, trying not to run.

She closed her door and leaned against it. Her reflection in the mirror opposite showed spots of colour burning in her pale face, and an almost feral glitter in her eyes.

Further protest was futile, and she knew it. Even if she locked herself in, and refused to go to the wedding, she couldn't win. Because no lock would be strong enough to keep him out, if he decided to impose his will on her, and she knew it.

'Damn him,' she said raggedly. 'Oh—damn him...'

CHAPTER TWELVE

KATE learned to smile that day. To smile at the aunts, uncles and cousins who embraced her and welcomed her so warmly to the family.

To smile at Ari when he said slowly, 'But what a vision, *pedhi mou*. A bride again yourself. Your husband is indeed a fortunate man.'

To smile as she stood beside Mick in the small incense-filled church, brilliant with candlelight and glittering with icons, and he took her hand in his. And the female members of both families sighed sentimentally, because they thought it was a gesture of love and he was remembering his own wedding day. Because they didn't know the truth—that it was all a pretence.

And to smile, at last, with genuine mistiness at Ismene, as she appeared, amid gasps and sighs from the onlookers, in her shimmering gown, her veil floating around her, to join her bridegroom.

It was a beautiful ceremony full of symbolism and ritual, and Ismene's voice was tremulous as she took her vows in front of the tall bearded priest. Petros was looking at her as if she was some goddess come to earth, and Kate felt tears prick her eyelids as she scattered handfuls of rice over the newly married pair at the conclusion of the marriage.

Afterwards musicians conducted Ismene and Petros to the square outside. It was festive in the sunlight, draped with bunting, and wreaths of flowers. Long tables had been set up, with platters of fish and chicken, bowls of salad and hummous, and still-warm loaves of bread. There was lamb roasting on spits, and tall jugs of local wine. The whole village

seemed to be in attendance, and there was a carnival atmosphere as they jostled for seats.

Kate realised that Mick was taking her to the top table, where the bride and groom were already ensconced. Victorine had not attended the church ceremony, but she was there now in a vivid yellow dress and a matching picture hat, fussing over where to sit.

Kate hung back. 'Please, I—I'd rather sit somewhere else.'

He said quietly, 'Kate, you are my wife, and you will take your proper place.'

'Well, my son,' Ari came up to them. 'Are you asking Katharina's forgiveness for having cheated her?'

There was a sudden roaring in her ears. She said faintly, 'What—did you say?'

But he'd turned back to Mick. 'Your wedding should have been like this. Not in some cold London office,' he chided jovially. 'But I was thinking, as I watched the children just now, that we should ask the good father to perform a blessing on your marriage, in the church with all of us to see. Kate would like that, *ne*?'

Kate murmured something faintly, and let Mick lead her away. She stole a glance at him, and saw that his face was grim, his mouth hard and set.

She said, with a catch in her voice, 'We can't go on like this. You must—say something.'

He said brusquely, 'I intend to.'

She saw an empty chair and took it, finding herself wedged between Dr Alessou and an elderly aunt, with a fierce stare and a diamond brooch like a sunburst.

She applauded as Petros and Ismene walked round the square, handing out sugared almonds from decorated baskets, and pretended to eat when the food was served. And she did not once look at Mick who was sitting further down the table, with Victorine beside him.

Was it intended as some kind of public declaration? she wondered. Had it begun?

It was good when the dancing started, and she had something she could focus on. The dancers wore traditional costume, the men in waistcoats and baggy breeches, with broad sashes and striped stockings, and the girls, their heads covered by scarves, in long skirts under flowered aprons, but there was no doubting the sheer athleticism of their performance.

And when they'd finished their exhibition, it was everyone else's turn. The dancers began to weave their way round the square, between the tables, pulling people up to join them in a long chain.

Kate saw Linda seized, laughing a protest as she went.

Then they reached her, and a plump woman in a red dress grabbed her hand, tugging her up in turn.

At first Kate felt clumsy—a fish out of water—as she tried to copy the intricate pattern of steps they were repeating over and over again, but the women holding her hands on either side were loud in their encouragement, and gradually the rhythm took over, and she was able to follow them with mounting confidence.

I used to do this kind of thing all the time when I was a rep, she thought. I'm just out of practice.

As the chain twisted and wove past the top table again, she saw Ari clapping enthusiastically, and Ismene and Petros beaming at her. And she saw Mick, his expression unreadable. And his companion, her beautiful face a mask of contempt.

To hell with her, Kate thought with sudden passion. To hell with both of them.

The sun was on her face, and the throb of the music had found an echo in her veins. In spite of herself, she was caught up in the sheer exuberance of the moment. The unexpected pleasure of belonging.

The rhythm changed, and she found herself dancing with a man from the village, linked to him by the coloured handkerchief he ceremoniously offered her.

She was breathless when the music eventually paused, and excused herself smilingly, amid protests.

She sank into her seat, grateful for the water that Dr Alessou poured for her.

'Why did he do that?' she asked, as she put down the empty glass. 'With the handkerchief, I mean? The other men are holding the women's hands.'

The doctor smiled at her. 'Because you are still a new wife, *kyria*, and it is believed that your hand should touch no other man's but your husband's.'

'Oh,' Kate said, and hastily poured herself some wine.

At sunset, the cars arrived to take the guests back to the villa, and the private evening party, but the celebrations in the village would clearly go on well into the night.

The *saloni* had been cleared for dancing, and there was more food laid out in the dining room.

Petros and Ismene opened the dancing, moving slowly to the music in each other's arms. Champagne was drunk, then Ari made a speech formally welcoming Petros to his family, and then the bride and groom were free to get changed and leave on their honeymoon.

Kate was at the back of the laughing throng that watched them depart, and she turned back with a sigh, wondering if it would be noticed if she too slipped away.

The music had resumed in the *saloni*, the small band playing something soft and dreamy, and people were heading back there. Kate went along with them, ostensibly part of the group, but separate, making her private plans.

She'd go out on the terrace as if she needed air, then take the steps at the end to get to the beach house. Where she would pack. She wouldn't be able to get off the island tonight, but she would leave first thing in the morning, and Mick would be free to do whatever he wanted. And she would not have to watch.

She began to move round the edge of the room, looking

down to avoid eye contact. Trying to be as unobtrusive as possible.

Only someone was barring the way. She raised unwilling eyes and saw Mick regarding her gravely.

He said quietly, 'Dance with me, *matia mou*.'

'In order to keep up appearances?' Kate lifted her chin. 'I think I'll sit this one out.'

'No,' he said. 'You will not. You have danced with everyone else today. Now it is my turn.' He took her hand and drew her on to the floor.

His arms enfolded her, holding her intimately against him, as they began to move to the music.

For a moment, Kate was rigid in his embrace. Her reason, the sudden clamour of her outraged senses were all telling her that this was a pretence too far. That she should not permit him to take this advantage.

Then, almost imperceptibly, she began to relax. To move with the flow, and go where the music and her husband's arms took her.

She felt the touch of his cheek against her hair. The swift brush of his mouth on her temple.

Even with that briefest of contacts, she felt her heartbeat hurry into madness. She felt the warm blood mantling her face. Was aware that her nipples had hardened in sweet, excruciating need against the silk that covered them.

And as if in response to some secret signal, Mick's arms tightened around her, his hand feathering across her spine, and his lips grazing the curve of her cheek, the corner of her trembling mouth.

With a little sigh of capitulation, Kate slid her arms up around his neck and buried her face in his shoulder.

She was no longer a separate entity, she realised, but part of him. Indivisibly. Unequivocally. Bound to him in some mysterious region of the senses where logic, commonsense—even decency—counted for nothing.

Where the only truth was that he was her man, and she

was his woman, and she would burn for him until the end of eternity.

She could count every day, every moment, every second that they had been apart. Recall every night when her imagination had brought him hauntingly back to her.

She could think of nothing—remember nothing—anticipate nothing but the glide of his hands on her naked skin delighting every pulse, every nerve. The lingering arousal of his mouth. The moment when her starved body would open to receive him.

She was dimly aware that the music had stopped—had been replaced by another sound.

As she raised her head uncertainly she realised with shock that she and Mick now had the floor to themselves, and the sound she could hear was applause from the other guests, clustering round to watch them in laughing, vociferous approval.

Bringing her back with a bump to sudden, stark reality.

Kate's face flamed in horrified embarrassment, and she tried to tug free, bent on flight, but Mick was holding her too firmly.

'Smile, *agapi mou*,' he murmured, acknowledging the plaudits with mocking self-deprecation.

She said between her teeth, as she obeyed, 'You'll stop at nothing, will you?'

'At very little, certainly.' He spun her round, away from him, then pulled her close, his lips taking hers in a brief hard kiss. 'And before tonight is over, you will be glad of it, my wife,' he added softly. 'This nonsense between us is over, and you are coming back to my bed where you belong.'

He released her, and she walked away from him, trying not to run. At the edge of the floor, she nearly collided with someone. She glanced up, her lips shaping an apology, and saw it was Victorine, her eyes glittering with malice and derision.

She held Kate's arms above the elbow, and leaned forward as if to embrace her.

'That was good, *chère*,' she breathed in her ear. 'What a pity Michalis has to run the Theodakis corporation. He would have made such a wonderful actor.'

Kate shook her off, uncaring who might see, and pushed past. She had to fight her way out of the room. Everyone wanted to speak to her, it seemed, and shake hands. But, at last, she won free, and found a quiet corner where she could recover her equilibrium a little.

She asked a passing waiter to bring her some fruit juice, and stood, sipping it, relishing its coolness against her parched throat, as Mick's parting words ran mad circles in her brain.

It was some new game he was playing. It had to be. He wasn't serious. He couldn't be. Because they had a deal. A bargain.

But all the same, she wouldn't waste any time getting away. Not the airport this time, but one of the ferries. It didn't matter which. Nothing mattered very much. Not any more.

And because of that, she could go back into the *saloni* this one last time, and act as the hostess. She could talk to people, and dance with anyone who asked her. And she would not— *not* let herself think of Mick's arms, and the familiar strength and urgency of his body.

No, she thought. She would never think of that again. And one day, her mind would have ground the image of him into such tiny particles that she would actually be able to forget him, and start to live again.

It was dawn before the party ended, and the last stalwarts made their way to their rooms, or were driven to the nearby hotels.

She saw Mick go into the study with his father, laughing, their arms round each other's shoulders, and drew a deep breath. She would never have a better opportunity.

She slid out of the house, and went down through the quiet pines to the beach house.

There was a chill in the air, heralding an autumn she would never see. And a chill in her heart that no sun could ever warm.

Once in her room, she drew a steadying breath. It was time to go.

She took Mick's diamonds from her ears and throat, and replaced them in their cases, then removed her wedding dress, and hung it back in the closet.

She would take with her only what she had brought, she decided, slipping on her robe, and fastening its sash.

She found her smallest travel bag, and began to fill it with underwear and shoes. She still had money left over from the Athens trip, and her car keys.

But not her passport, she realised with sudden dismay. Mick had that. She could remember him slipping it into the inside pocket of the jacket he'd been wearing.

Oh, let it still be there, she thought with panic. Don't let him have locked it in the desk up at the villa.

She trod barefoot down the passage, and went into his room, trying unsuccessfully to remember which coat it had been. Well, she would simply have to look in all of them, she thought sighing. Starting with the one hanging on the back of the chair.

'Tidying up for me, *agapi mou*?' His voice from the doorway behind her made her jump, and she whirled, holding his jacket against her like a shield. 'Maria will complain.'

He came further into the room, and kicked the door shut behind him. He was in his shirt sleeves, his tie hanging loose, his coat slung over one shoulder. And he was smiling.

He said softly, 'So you are here at last.'

'No,' she said. 'You—you're mistaken. I came to look for something.'

'And so did I.' He tossed his jacket and tie on to the empty

chair, and began to unbutton his shirt, his eyes never leaving hers.

'What are you doing?' Her voice sounded high, unnatural.

'Taking off my clothes. I usually do before I go to bed. And then, *matia mou*, I shall undress you.'

Kate backed away. 'Don't come near me,' she said hoarsely.

'But that wouldn't work.' He dropped his shirt to the floor, and unzipped his pants. 'For what I intend, my Kate, we need to be gloriously, intimately close. As we used to be, such a short time ago. Before I made you angry and you decided you hated me.'

She said passionately, 'But I do hate you. And I am not— *not* going to allow you to do this.'

He sighed. 'Kate, I was your lover for six exquisite months. I know your body as well as I know my own. I can feel your response when I touch you, and while we were dancing tonight, you wanted me.'

'No.' She wanted the denial to be fierce, but instead it sounded as if she was pleading. 'You can't do this.'

'I must,' he said almost gently. 'Because without you, *agapi mou*, I am dying inside. I need you to heal me. To make me whole again.'

He took her in his arms, the naked heat of his body permeating her thin robe.

He said softly, 'Don't fight me, Kate. I am so very tired of fighting.' And then he kissed her.

His lips were a seduction in themselves, moving warmly and persuasively on hers, coaxing them apart, while his hands untied her sash, and pushed the concealing robe from her shoulders. Her eyes closed and she surrendered, allowing him the access he desired to the sweet moisture of her mouth.

Then he lifted her, and carried her to the bed, lying beside her as his long supple fingers began to rediscover her. And the scraps of silk and lace she was wearing were no barrier at all.

When he kissed her again, she responded swiftly, ardently, making her own feverish demands.

The tips of her bared breasts grazed his chest. Her hands sought him. Enclosed him.

And she felt, in her turn, the shiver of his touch on her thighs, and heard herself moan softly in need.

He whispered, 'No, *agapi mou*. You take me.'

And he turned on to his back, lifting her above him. Over him.

Her possession of him was slow and sweet, her body closing round him like the petals of a flower as she filled herself with him deeply, gloriously.

And he lay watching her, the breath catching in his throat as he caressed her, his fingertips brushing subtly across her flesh, making the pink nipples pucker and lift.

His hands stroked the length of her body from her shoulders to her flanks, and back again, tracing the vulnerable curve of her spine so that her body arched in sudden delight.

She began to move on him slowly, savouring every distinct, separate sensation, then increased the rhythm, hearing his breathing change as she did so.

She controlled him like a moon with a tidal sea, using her body like an instrument to bring him pleasure.

And then, before she was even prepared for it, all control was gone, and their locked bodies were straining frantically together seeking a consummation.

She heard him gasp her name, and answered him wordlessly as they took each other over the edge, and down into the abyss.

Afterwards, he slept in her arms, and she held him, as the slow tears edged out from under her lashes, and scalded her face.

Then quietly, inch by inch, she eased herself away from him, towards the edge of the bed. She found her robe, and put it on, then retrieved her underwear.

Moving gingerly, she opened the closet door, and began to search through his clothes for her passport.

It was nearly ten minutes before she found it. Ten precious moments of early morning turning into broad daylight, and increasing the risk of discovery.

She took one last look at Mick's sleeping figure.

She thought, 'Goodbye, my love' and knew that her heart was weeping. Then she slipped quietly out of the door, and back to her room.

She collected fresh undies, and a straight cream skirt with a black short-sleeved top, then went into the bathroom to shower and dress, and collect her toiletries.

The house was still quiet, and there was no sign of Maria. Maybe everyone was sleeping late today. So far, so good, thought Kate and went quickly and cautiously across the passage and into her room.

Mick was standing by the window. He'd dressed in denim pants and a polo shirt, and his arms were folded across his chest.

She halted, her throat closing in panic. She said huskily, 'I thought you were asleep.'

'I missed you beside me,' he said. 'And it woke me.'

He looked from her to the hastily packed travel bag, his mouth curling.

He said quietly, 'Were you planning to leave me another note, Katharina? What would this one have said, I wonder?'

'The same as the last one.' She flung back her head. 'That our marriage was a mistake, and I can't stay with you.'

'Nor can you leave,' he said. 'Not now. Because a little while ago, we may have given our child life.'

She stared at him. 'No.' Her voice shook. 'That's—not possible.'

He sighed. 'You cannot be that naïve. But the point is this. I want to make a baby with you, if not now, then in the future. And I intend our child to grow up with both parents.'

She said slowly, 'You want a child? But why now—of all

times? You've always refused to consider it before.' She paused. 'Oh, I understand. I suppose my replacement doesn't want to be pregnant. Doesn't want to spoil her wonderful figure. So, you'll just use me instead.' She gave a small, hysterical laugh. 'My God, I should have seen that coming.'

He said impatiently, 'You're talking like a crazy woman. What replacement in the name of God?' He didn't wait for an answer. 'But if you want to know why I hesitated over a baby, it was because I was scared.'

'You—scared?' Kate stared up at him in patent unbelief. 'Oh what, pray?'

He said roughly, 'Of losing you, *pedhi mou*, as I lost my mother. If she had not given birth to Ismene and myself, she could have been alive today. But the strain of it weakened her heart.'

'And you thought that might happen to me? That's absurd.' She lifted her chin. 'I prefer my own version. That you want a child, and you know Victorine won't give you one.'

'Victorine?' he repeated. 'What does she have to do with all this.'

'She's your mistress.' At last she'd made herself say the word. 'And she's going to be your wife, once you've got rid of me and taken over the company. So there's no room for me. And if I am having a baby, I'm damned if I'll surrender it to you to bring up—with her. The stepmother from hell.'

Mick said slowly, 'Why, in the name of God, should I marry Victorine? Yes, we were involved—once. You knew that. But it is long over. And will never be resumed.'

She said, 'That isn't true. Because you were here with her—on the day you came back from the States. When you thought I was in Ithaca. I *found* you together, both of you naked. In—that other room. In that bed—where we...' She couldn't finish the sentence.

He stared at her. 'You—found us having sex?'

'No,' Kate said. 'It was just the aftermath, but it had the same kind of punch. You were asleep on the bed, and she'd

been having a shower. Neither of you were wearing any clothes.' Her voice shook. 'She—suggested I should—knock in future.'

He was very still. 'So, possessing this indisputable evidence, maybe you would prefer it if I left, and took Victorine with me.'

'I don't think she'd go.'

'No?' His smile chilled her. 'Well, let us see.'

He took Kate by the wrist, and marched her to the door. She struggled a little.

'Let me go. Where are you taking me?'

'We're going up to the villa,' he said. 'To ask her.'

CHAPTER THIRTEEN

'MICK, you can't do this.' Kate stumbled in his wake as he strode up the track towards the villa. 'You'll ruin everything for yourself. Lose everything you've worked for.'

'You speak as if that matters,' he threw over his shoulder at her. 'There are worse losses.'

'But think what it will do to your father,' she panted. 'Even if he did take her away from you, he doesn't deserve that kind of humiliation.'

'Now there we differ. A man who does that deserves everything he gets.' He walked into the villa's hallway, pulling Kate behind him, and paused. 'I presume they will still be in their suite at this time.'

'Yes,' she said. 'But please stop and think before you go in there.'

'What is there to think about?' Mick swung round, his eyes blazing. 'According to you, my passion for Victorine has corrupted my mind—my sense of honour. Therefore, I no longer have to consider the consequences of my actions.'

Kate said shakily, 'In that case, I'd rather stay here.'

'But you cannot,' he said. 'Because this is the moment when all your reasons for leaving me will be totally confirmed. When your condemnation of me for a liar and an adulterer will be completely justified.

'So, you should be there, *agapi mou*. It is not something you can afford to miss. Come.'

Kate went with him because she had no choice. She was trembling as he knocked imperatively at his father's door, and heard him call, 'Enter.'

They found Ari lying on the sofa, in dressing gown and

178

pyjamas, reading a newspaper, with a pot of coffee beside him.

He put down his book and studied them frowning slightly. 'Is this not a little early for social calls? All our guests are still asleep.'

'I am aware of that,' Mick said brusquely. 'But I have a matter to deal with which will not wait. I need to speak to Victorine urgently.'

Ari's frown deepened. 'She is also sleeping. Perhaps I can give her a message for you—at some more reasonable time?'

'No,' Mick said. 'I need to talk to her. We have been having a passionate affair behind your back, you understand, and I have decided to ask her to go away with me.'

Kate folded her arms across her body, feeling suddenly sick. She waited for the explosion, but it didn't come.

Instead, Ari said composedly, 'I see now why this cannot wait. I will fetch her.'

He rose and went into the bedroom and, a few minutes later, Victorine emerged. She was wearing a black lace night-gown with a matching peignoir clutched round her.

Her hair was a mess and Kate noticed with pleasure that her eyes were puffy.

'What is this, *cher*?' She seated herself on the sofa, disposing her draperies with conscious elegance. She was smiling, but her eyes were wary. 'Ari says you want me.'

'More than life itself, it seems,' Mick said. 'So much so, that I have wrecked my marriage for you. And now I am here to put an end to all this hidden passion and deceit, and admit our love openly.'

Victorine stiffened. She said. 'What are you talking about? Have you gone mad?'

'I have simply decided that nothing matters more than our love.' Mick shrugged. 'Naturally, I shall have to resign from the Theodakis Corporation, when the press learn the truth. But that will simply give me more time to devote to you, my dear Victorine, and your career. It is fortunate that you have

an alternative source of income. I have become used to certain standards.'

He smiled blandly at her. 'So, if you will pack your things, we can be leaving.'

She said hoarsely, '*Tu es fou.* You are crazy—or drunk. What nonsense is this?'

'No nonsense, my sweet. Have you forgotten that Kate found us enjoying an illicit afternoon of love together? I think—I really think you should have mentioned to me that she saw us. It explains so much.'

Victorine looked at Kate, her face ugly. 'She is lying,' she said. 'She is trying to make trouble for me.' She turned to Ari, who was standing beside her, his face expressionless. '*Cher*, you do not believe this ridiculous story?'

'You were in our bedroom,' Kate said steadily. 'Mick was asleep, and you were combing your hair. You had a towel on, and nothing else. And you told me to knock in future.'

'No.' Victorine's voice rose. 'None of this is true. You are making it up—to blacken me in Ari's eyes. But it will not work.'

'Are you telling me you have forgotten it all?' Mick asked reproachfully. 'The passion we shared? The promises we made to each other?'

Victorine transferred her glare to him. 'I am saying it did not happen,' she returned shrilly.

'It was the day Mick came back from New York,' Kate continued. An immense calm seemed to have settled on her. 'I was supposed to go to Ithaca, and Mick's father had gone fishing with a friend. But my trip was cancelled, and when I rang home, Yannis told me that Mick was here. So, I came rushing back to the beach house to see him. Only, I found you as well.' For the first time there was a break in her voice.

'A terrible betrayal.' Ari's tone was meditative. 'We have both been deceived, Katharina.' He paused. 'Is this why you went back to England so suddenly, *pedhi mou*?'

'Yes.' Kate bit her lip.

'Without speaking of what you had seen—or demanding an explanation from my son?'

'I couldn't say anything. It was too painful. And there was no reason for anyone else to be hurt,' she added with difficulty. 'Besides, the evidence was there. I know what I saw.'

'So, you decided to spare my feelings at the expense of your own.' Ari nodded thoughtfully. 'That was kind, my child, but unnecessary. I have long known the truth.'

He looked at Mick. 'What happened that afternoon, my son?'

'I wish I knew.' Mick shrugged. 'I returned from New York earlier than planned, but when I arrived Yannis told me Kate had gone out for the day.

He frowned. 'I went down to the house to change. The jet lag had hit me hard, so I tried taking a shower. In the end, I decided to have a brief nap. I remember nothing more.'

He looked at Kate. 'Except that at some point you touched me, and said my name. I suppose you were trying to wake me. And I said "I love you."'

Kate's eyes widened, and her hand went to her throat.

'But when I eventually awoke,' he went on almost conversationally. 'It was to find you had left me—with a note simply stating our marriage was over.'

His mouth twisted. 'I assumed that you were still angry about my refusal to take you to New York—and that other disagreement we'd had.

'But I couldn't believe you'd gone without giving me a chance to put things right between us, and so I got angry too.

'But, of course, I didn't realise you'd discovered my flagrant infidelity,' he added reflectively. 'Little wonder that you did not wish to remain with me.'

'Ari,' Victorine spoke desperately. 'Don't listen to them. This is all nonsense. You heard—their marriage is in deep trouble, and because of that they are trying to destroy our relationship too.'

'What I see,' Ari said, 'Is that something happened that afternoon that was sufficient to put Katharina to flight. To

make her wish to end her marriage to my son. And that is serious.

'Or perhaps not,' he added meditatively. 'Maybe it was intended as a joke—only it misfired a little.' He looked at Victorine. 'Is that how it was, *kougla mou*?'

His voice was gentle, but there was a note in it that sent a shiver down Kate's spine.

There was a long taut silence, then Victorine said sullenly, 'A joke, yes. But she was too stupid to realise she was being teased,' she added with a venomous look at Kate.

'I see.' Ari nodded. 'But why did you not explain this good joke as soon as you saw that it had gone wrong? That it had caused real hurt? Because you must have realised this very quickly.'

There was another silence, then Victorine shrugged defensively. 'They were—neither of them here. Michalis was working, and the girl was in London.'

'The girl?' Mick's voice bit. 'You will speak of my wife with respect.'

'What is there to respect?' Victorine spat back at him, her face twisted, ugly with dislike. 'She has nothing—is nothing—that pale-faced English bitch. What has she to offer any man? And you—you could have had me.'

There was another telling silence, then Mick said gently, 'There was never any question of marriage between us, Victorine, and I made that clear to you from the first. If you believed that might change, I am sorry.'

'Sorry.' She threw back her head and laughed harshly, the creamy skin tinged with an unhealthy flush. 'Yes, you have been sorry, Kyrios Theodakis, as you deserve. Because no man ever finishes with me. I am the one who leaves—always. Always—do you hear me?'

'Is that what this was all about?' Mick closed his eyes for a second. 'Dear God, it is unbelievable.'

'And then your wife left you,' Victorine went on gloatingly. 'So you found out what it was like. Oh, that made me happy.' And she laughed again.

'Please.' Kate's voice was barely audible. 'I don't think I can bear any more of this.'

'You do not have to, *pedhi mou*. None of us do.' There was a cold harshness in Ari's voice. He looked at Mick, 'Go with your wife, my son. Make things right between you.'

He paused. 'But first be good enough to ask Iorgos Vasso to come here. There are arrangements to be made. And send Androula also,' he added. 'Victorine will need help with her packing.'

'You are telling me to go?' Victorine's voice cracked.

'*Ne*,' he said. 'As I should have done long ago.' He gave a bitter sigh. 'I was wrong to bring you here, and I knew it. It was an act of stupidity and vindictiveness by a man who had quarrelled with his son.' He looked at Mick. 'You made me feel old, Michalis, and I did not wish that. I wanted my youth back again—my strength. But I have learned my lesson.'

'You can send me away—after all we have been to each other?' Victorine's tone was pleading.

'You are a beautiful woman, Victorine. And I am a rich fool. It is not a very admirable combination. But, let us not waste time in recrimination,' he added more briskly. 'Iorgos will arrange to have you flown anywhere you wish to go.'

She stumbled to her feet. 'Yes,' she said thickly. 'You are a fool—to think that I could ever want you. It was Michalis—always. Can't you see that? I thought if I came here, I could make him want me again.'

'Yes,' Ari said quietly. 'He saw that, but I would not, and we quarrelled again. But now it is all over. And you, *kougla mou*, will have to find another rich fool.'

'But then he brought *her*,' Victorine went on as if he had not spoken. 'And I saw the way he looked at her, and spoke. I knew that he loved her, and I wished to destroy that. I was there when Yannis took her call, so I went down to the beach house and found Michalis asleep.' She gave a throaty giggle. 'It was perfect. All I had to do was undress also—and wait.'

Kate pressed her knuckles against her mouth. 'Oh, God.'

Mick's arm was round her, holding her as she swayed. 'Come, *agapi mou*. You don't need to hear any more. Let us go back to the house.'

'Look after her,' Ari called after them. 'But do not forget that we have guests. I need Katharina to preside at the breakfast table.'

'Then you will be disappointed, Papa,' Michael tossed back at him. 'Do not expect either of us until dinner.'

In the hallway, he said, 'I must find Iorgos, and Androula. Will you wait for me?'

'Yes,' she said. 'I'll wait.'

He framed her face with his hands, looking into her eyes. 'And you won't run away from me again?'

Her lips trembled into a smile. 'Not this time. I'll be on the terrace.'

Outside, the wind was fresh and clean. Kate leaned on the balustrade, looking down at the foam-capped waves through the trees.

He came to stand beside her. 'What are you thinking?'

She said, with a shiver, 'That was—horrible.'

'Perhaps.' He shrugged. 'But also effective.'

'I almost feel sorry for her.'

'Save your compassion, my Kate. She showed no pity for you.'

Kate hesitated. 'Whatever she's done, she *is* very beautiful. Were you ever in love with her?'

'No,' he said quietly. 'I found her amusing at first, but I soon realised that her loveliness was only skin deep. I ended the relationship without regret.'

'How on earth did your father get involved with her?'

'To spite me,' he said wryly. 'You heard what he said, *matia mou*. They met at a party, not by chance, I am sure, and somehow she convinced him that she had ditched me, not the other way around, and that she found younger men boring.'

He grimaced. 'At the time, it was what he wanted to hear. He was very lonely when my mother died, and Linda had

become, perhaps, too much part of the household. A companion for Ismene rather than himself.'

He sighed. 'I knew what she was, and tried to warn him. But that was a disaster. He said that I was jealous because she'd found him the better man. I could have dealt with that, but then Victorine started to make him jealous by coming on to me.' He shook his head. 'It was a nightmare.'

She said neutrally, 'So—you needed a wife. An answer to your problem.'

'If you remember,' he said softly. 'I said you would create more problems than you would solve. And how right I was.' He tutted reprovingly. 'Fighting with me. Refusing to be demure and obedient like a good Greek wife.'

'Is that what you wanted?'

'I wanted you, *agapi mou*.' He put his arm round her, as they walked down the steps to the track. 'From that first moment. Did you think it was a coincidence I turned up in London?' He shook his head. 'It was not. I came to find you.'

He gave her a swift, sidelong glance. 'If I am honest, I am not sure I intended marriage, not at first. But long before we made love, I knew that I could not live without you.'

'And yet you went to New York on your own.'

'Yes,' he said. 'And missed you like hell at every moment. Is that what you wanted to hear? That's why I came back early—to tell you that I was all kinds of a fool, and ask you to forgive me. And promise that I would never go anywhere without you again.'

He was silent for a moment. 'I also knew that I had to tell you why I'd been reluctant for us to have a baby. That it wasn't fair to hide my fears from you. Only, I wasn't used to having to explain myself—or to being married.'

'You will have to make allowances for me, *agapi mou*,' he added ruefully.

'When I awoke and found you gone, I felt as if someone had ripped out my heart. I wanted to come after you right away, but I told myself I should give you a chance to cool down—to miss me a little.'

'And instead, I asked for a divorce.'

'That,' he said quietly, 'was the worst day of my life. I kept asking myself how this could have happened? How I could have lost you. And began to come up with answers I did not want.'

'What sort of answers?'

He sighed. 'A friend of mine on Corfu met a girl on holiday,' he said reluctantly. 'The marriage lasted a year, then she went back to England, and took their child. She told him she had never loved him, and never wished to live in Greece. It was only his money she wanted. The divorce settlement.'

Kate gasped. 'And you thought that I—I was the same?' She tried to pull away from him. 'Oh, how could you?'

But he held her firmly. 'When you are hurt and angry, anything seems possible,' he told her levelly. 'And after all, my Kate, you had never once told me you loved me.'

She said breathlessly, 'But you knew how I felt. You must have done.'

'I knew you liked being in bed with me.' His tone was wry. 'But I needed more. I wanted you to speak the words.'

'Well, you didn't say them either,' Kate pointed out. 'Or not until that dreadful afternoon—and even then I thought you'd mistaken me for Victorine.'

'However deeply asleep I was, I would always hear your voice, *agapi mou*. Know your touch, and no other. Every soul in this world could see that I was crazy for you—even Victorine,' he added soberly.

She shivered. 'And she nearly destroyed us. Oh, Mick, happiness is such a fragile thing.'

'Together, we will make it strong.' He lifted her up into his arms and carried her over the threshold of the beach house.

'Our marriage begins again here,' he told her softly. 'I love you so much, my Kate.'

'Yes.' She smiled up at him, her eyes luminous. 'And I love you, Michalis *mou*. Now and for ever.'

'For ever,' he whispered. And kissed her.

International
bestselling author

Miranda
LEE

Brings you the final three
novels in her famous
Hearts of Fire miniseries...

FORTUNE *&* **FATE**

The passion, scandal and
hopes of Australia's
fabulously wealthy
Whitmore family promise
riveting reading in this
special volume containing
three full-length novels.

*Available in January 2003 at
your favorite retail outlet.*

If you enjoyed what you just read,
then we've got an offer you can't resist!

Take 2 bestselling love stories FREE!

Plus get a FREE surprise gift!

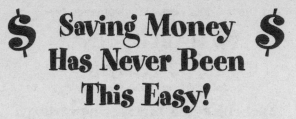

$ Saving Money $
Has Never Been
This Easy!

Just fill out and send in this form from any
October, November and December 2002 books
and we will send you a coupon booklet worth a
total savings of $20.00 off future purchases of
Harlequin and Silhouette books in 2003.

Yes! It's that easy!

I accept your incredible offer!
Please send me a coupon booklet:

Name (PLEASE PRINT)

Address   Apt. #

City   State/Prov.   Zip/Postal Code

In a typical month, how many
Harlequin and Silhouette novels do you read?

❏ 0-2   ❏ 3+

097KJKDNC7   097KJKDNDP

Please send this form to:
In the U.S.: Harlequin Books, P.O. Box 9071, Buffalo, NY 14269-9071
In Canada: Harlequin Books, P.O. Box 609, Fort Erie, Ontario L2A 5X3

Allow 4-6 weeks for delivery. Limit one coupon booklet per household. Must be
postmarked no later than January 15, 2003.

HARLEQUIN®
Makes any time special ®

Silhouette®
Where love comes alive™

© 2002 Harlequin Enterprises Limited

PHQ402

Season's Greetings

from

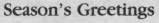

Seduction and Passion Guaranteed!

The world's bestselling romance series.

Treat yourself to a gift this Christmas!

Enjoy these holiday stories,
written especially for you:

CHRISTMAS EVE WEDDING
by Penny Jordan #2289

CHRISTMAS AT HIS COMMAND
by Helen Brooks #2292

THE PLAYBOY'S MISTRESS
by Kim Lawrence #2294

All on sale in December

Pick up a Harlequin Presents® novel
and you will enter a world of
spine-tingling passion and provocative,
tantalizing romance!

Available wherever Harlequin books are sold.

HARLEQUIN®
Makes any time special®